WANT FREE SEDONA VENEZ BOOKS?

Sign up for Sedona Venez's Newsletter and receive FREE BOOKS. In addition to the free stories, you will also get special pricing, exclusive previews and news of new releases.

GET A FREE SEDONA VENEZ BOOK!

Join Sedona's mailing list to be the first to know of new releases, free books, special prices and other author giveaways.

https://sedonavenez.com/free-book

HUNTER

WOLF ELITE SHIFTERS

SEDONA VENEZ

HUNTER

"HUNTER, so are you going to hang out with me at the blackjack table all night or what?"

I scowled at Matt, who had spoken to me out of the corner of his mouth while he dealt the fiftieth round of blackjack for the night. Matt had become a professional poker player when he, Eli, Gunner, Jordan, and I were all discharged from the Army, and I could see why. He'd won more than half of the rounds he'd dealt tonight.

"Maybe I'm just trying to stick it out until I actually beat your ass," I muttered while peeking at my cards.

This earned me a glare from my friend, but I didn't care. It wasn't like Matt was really going to kick me off the table or anything. I'd dropped a fair bit of money during the game tonight, and besides, we'd been friends for too damn long.

We played another round, which I lost badly after busting on a double down, before Matt spoke again, "That blonde over by the pool table has been eyeing you all night."

I stifled a sigh and fought not to glance in that direction. "I know."

Matt raised an eyebrow, though he didn't look my way. "You know there's a hot chick across the room who's been salivating to take a bite out of your ass, and you're still sitting here?"

I gritted my teeth, suddenly annoyed. "Maybe she's looking at you."

"Damn, Hunter. Have you gone soft on me?" Matt chuckled, returning his attention to the game.

I growled, finally gave in, and turned my attention toward the pool table area across the casino floor. Sure enough, the blonde was still there, playing pool with her brunette friend. I watched as she leaned over the table in her tight silver dress, and my cock hardened as her breasts nearly spilled out of the low neckline.

I licked my lips as she positioned her cue, and just before she took the shot, she turned her head and winked at me.

Hot damn. I could really get behind that.

She's trash, my inner wolf growled.

I gritted my teeth as my beast's disgust trickled through me. Instantly, my hard-on started to deflate.

You're not sticking our cock in that.

Our cock? I seethed indignantly. *The last time I checked, my dick wasn't covered in fur.*

Nevertheless, we still inhabit the same body, my wolf argued. *And that woman over there is trash.*

I sighed heavily. I hadn't thought wolves had such high standards. Luck would have it that I'd get a beast with the heart of a woman.

Why does my wolf give a shit if the blonde is easy?

She was ready and willing. And she was hot as hell and didn't look like she had an IQ much higher than 110. Those had been my requirements for taking a woman to bed for as long as I could remember, and I sure as hell wasn't going to change them now.

Not to mention, I deserved to blow off some steam after all the hell Eli had recently put me through with his Mafia bullshit. I'd worried myself to death over the whole thing for the last two months. And now that Eli was safe with his mate, Olivia, in New York City, I damn well deserved a breather. I didn't care what my high and mighty wolf thought. I was going to get laid tonight.

"See you," I told Matt, tossing my cards on the table as I stood up. "I've got better things to do."

"About time," Matt muttered. He flashed me a quick grin. "Going for the blonde?"

"Hell no. I'm going for both."

Not waiting for Matt's response, I sauntered over to the pool table with a lazy grin on my face, snagging two glasses of champagne from a passing cigarette girl as I went by.

"You girls have been playing for a while," I said, leaning my hip against the pool table. "Thought you could use a break."

"Oh, thanks." The blonde took the glass

from my hand with a smile, and tossing her curls back, she took a long drink.

The brunette, who wore a red sheath dress and had twisted her hair up into a sleek knot, was a little more conservative, preferring to slowly sip her drink. "I love champagne."

"So, who's winning?" I asked, coming around the table to the brunette's side. I held back a grin at the flash of jealousy in the blonde's green eyes, which I'd been counting on.

"I am," the blonde said, perching her dainty hand on her hips. Her fingernails sparkled in the light, painted the exact same shade as her dress. "I'm stripes."

I raised a brow as I surveyed the table. There were five solid balls and only two striped ones left. "Impressive." I grinned and then leaned over the brunette, who was getting ready to take her next shot. I wanted to test the boundaries, see if she was game for what I had in mind. "Here, let me help you with that," I said, sliding my hand along the cue. "You're going for the yellow ball, right?"

"Yeah," she replied.

I shifted subtly, pressing my hard-on against

her ass, and she rewarded me by pushing her shapely bottom back up against my groin.

Good girl.

No, my inner beast began.

But I shoved my wolf firmly into the back of my mind and erected a mental brick wall between my animal half and me. Blessed silence filled my head, and I nearly sighed with relief when no unwanted emotions flooded through me.

Time to play.

"Good. Raise your elbow just a little bit," I murmured in her ear, "and place your fingers just so." I adjusted her hand. "Now, you go ahead and take that shot, beautiful."

She did, and the yellow ball ricocheted off the side and then rolled neatly into the left corner pocket. "I did it!" the brunette exclaimed, jumping up as I stepped back. "You're a good teacher," she purred, her smoky eyes drinking me in.

"That's not fair." The blonde pouted, jutting out her pink lower lip as she crossed her arms beneath her breasts.

This time, I caught a flash of areola peeking out from the silvery fabric.

"I didn't get any help."

"Oh, I don't think you need any help, sweetheart," I said, hooking my arm around the blonde's waist. "You're clearly a woman who has no problem standing on her own two feet."

The blonde preened at that, flashing her friend a cheeky smile.

The brunette scowled, sidling closer. "I might not be good at pool, but at least I don't—"

"Now, now, ladies," I interrupted before a fight could break out. "No need to say anything you might regret. I'm not going to insult either of you by favoring one over the other, if you get my meaning." I grinned. "You're both far too beautiful for that."

The two women exchanged glances and then turned toward me with twin feline smiles.

"I have a hot tub in my suite," the brunette drawled. "What do you say we all have a nice, hot soak to...relax?"

"It would be my pleasure." Taking both ladies by their arms, I sauntered toward the elevator, making sure to pass by Matt's table so I could wink at the smug bastard on my way out.

~

"Ooh, yes, let me see that curvy ass," I growled, leaning against the rim of the hot tub as I watched the blonde slowly enter the water.

She was wearing an emerald-green bikini with a halter top that pushed her large breasts together, forming a glorious display of cleavage. My cock was harder than the Rock of Gibraltar, and nothing was going to stop me from finally releasing all of my pent-up sexual frustration.

The blonde slipped off her bikini bottoms and turned around, resting her elbows against the edge of the hot tub and lifting her ass into the air.

"Jesus." I whistled, reaching forward and grabbing each cheek. I squeezed hard. "You're gorgeous."

The brunette joined us, dressed in a red bikini that was little more than a crisscross of spaghetti straps covering her nipples and crotch.

"She likes it when you play with her nipples," the brunette said, surprising me while also telling me this was not their first rodeo together.

Smiling, I sat back and watched as the brunette turned the blonde around and started sucking on her left nipple. The blonde moaned, her hand wandering down to touch her bare pussy, her fingers glistening as they massaged her clit.

Oh, fuck yes! This is something straight out of a damn porno flick. How lucky can I possibly get?

I watched them fool around for a few moments. Then I stood and waded through the water toward them, wanting to get in on the action. "Come on over here, darling," I ordered the blonde, gently tugging on her hair, a clear sign of what I wanted.

She did as I asked, and as the brunette came around the other side of me to fondle my balls, I leaned back into the water and groaned.

This is heaven. Why haven't I thought of blocking off my beast before?

It had been so long. I hadn't had sex since Gunner's wedding night. The realization pushed me to the limit. I couldn't wait any longer. I reached over and grabbed a condom, ripping it out and rolling it onto my cock.

"Get on top of me," I growled, snatching the blonde up by the waist.

She squealed with delight as I pulled her out of the water and on top of me, positioning her entrance over the head of my cock.

Yes...this is fucking happening.

She slid onto me, engulfing me with her tight sheath, and my wolf beast broke through my mental shield with a resounding...

No!

Rage and disgust from my animal half flooded me, and my cock instantly went flaccid.

"Oh, hell no!" I roared, jolting up.

The blonde shrieked, scrambled off of me, and retreated to the other side of the hot tub. The brunette joined her, and both of them looked at me as if I were insane. I braced myself on the edge of the tub, panting hard, trying to get my emotions under control.

"What the hell was that?" the blonde demanded, her green eyes sparking fire. She hesitated, biting down on her bottom lip. "Did we do something wrong?"

"No," I bit out the word, hating the guilt I felt at causing these gorgeous women any kind of insecurity about themselves. "It's not you. It's me. I..."

What the hell can I say to them? That I am impotent?

Rage smoldered in my core at the very idea, and my cheeks burned with humiliation. I wanted to throttle my beast for putting me in this fucked-up predicament.

You wouldn't be in this situation if you'd just stayed at the poker table in the first place, my inner wolf pointed out smugly.

Why you little— I started when my cell rang, interrupting me.

I leaped out of the water, grateful for the distraction. "Sorry, ladies, I've got to take this." I wrapped a towel around my waist as I stepped out of the bathroom, suddenly uncomfortable with the idea of being naked around two women I couldn't fuck.

Gritting my teeth, I snatched up my cell that I'd left in the living room.

"Hello?" I snapped.

"Hunter." My brother Eric's voice burst through the other end. "God, I'm so glad I reached you. It's terrible."

"What? Are stock prices plummeting?" I asked sarcastically.

My brother rarely ever called for matters not having to do with money and business.

"Don't be an ass. It's Daniel Nash." Eric paused. "I just heard the news, and I know how close the two of you used to be, so I thought I should tell you."

"Old Daniel?" Dread filled my stomach at the mention of the rancher who had treated me like his son. "What's wrong?"

"He's dead."

❦ 2 ❧

KIA

"Kia! Phone call for you."

I bit back a snappy retort as I adjusted the focus on my camera lens. "Little busy here, Drew," I said. Then I lifted my head, so I could look at the basically nude model I was photographing. "Turn your head slightly to the left."

The model, who was wearing nothing but strategically placed paint, did as I had asked. I studied the play of light against her angular body and then dropped my gaze back down to the viewfinder.

"I told the lawyer on the phone you were in the middle of a shoot, but he was most insistent," Drew said, now hovering at my elbow.

I frowned, adjusting the aperture. "A lawyer? What the hell does he want?"

It'd better not be another lawsuit.

I'd gone through a nasty one several years ago, back when I was still doing wedding photography. I'd learned a big lesson back then. Even if you were an expert photographer and did an incredible job, you could still get royally screwed by your client.

"He said something about a great-uncle dying and an inheritance."

I nearly knocked over the tripod as I whirled around to face Drew. "Is this some kind of a joke?" I demanded. "I don't have a great-uncle."

Drew shrugged. "I don't know, but the guy sounds legit to me."

I sighed.

Despite Drew's purple hair and neck tattoos, which somehow managed not to clash with the dressy pants, button-up shirt, and vest he typically wore to work, he was the best assistant I'd ever hired and was damn good at weeding out the bullshit in my life. If he said the lawyer's call was legit, then it probably was.

"Tell him I'll be there in ten minutes."

It was more like twenty-five before I finally finished the shoot. As the model traded in her stilettos for a white silk bathrobe, I hightailed it to my office at the rear of the studio, my black-heeled boots clicking against the concrete floor of the warehouse I'd converted into my photography studio over a year ago. My mind spun with all the questions I'd pushed to the back of my mind while I was working.

Who is this great-uncle? What did he leave behind? How come I never knew him?

"I told him you'd call him back," Drew said from his desk as I stepped inside.

The office was a small glass and concrete structure I spent little time in since the majority of my after-shoot work occurred in the darkroom.

Drew pointed toward the phone perched on my desk without looking up from what he was doing. "You'll find the phone number on the sticky note I left there for you."

"Thanks." I dropped into my desk chair and then picked up the sticky note. I scowled as I read the phone number. "Area code 325? Where the hell is that?"

"Texas, I think," Drew said absently. "The guy on the phone had an accent thicker than a bowl of oatmeal." He glanced over at me. "Why? What's up?"

"I think I know who this is," I said slowly. Then I picked up the phone and dialed.

Drew started to ask more questions, but I tuned him out, letting the buzz of the ringtone fill my mind. My father's family was from Texas.

"Stafford Law," a woman with a Texas drawl answered pleasantly. "How may I help you?"

"Hi." I cleared my throat. "I'm calling for..." I checked the sticky note. "James Stafford. He just called my office a few minutes ago. My name is Kia Nash."

"Oh!" I heard papers shuffling in the background. "Yes, Mr. Stafford very much wants to speak with you, Miss Nash. Hold on just a moment."

There was silence for a minute, and then a gravelly, deep voice came on the line. "Kia Nash?"

"That's me." I tried to keep the impatience out of my voice. My nerves felt as though they'd been scraped raw already. "Are you the attorney who was trying to reach me?"

"Yes, Miss Nash." The lawyer coughed slightly. "I'm sorry to be the bearer of bad news, but I'm calling to inform you that your great-uncle Daniel Nash has passed away."

Daniel Nash. So, that was his name. I felt an unexpected lump form in my throat at the loss of a man I never knew, and I rolled my eyes. *Oh, who are you kidding? You never tried to seek out any family before. Get your shit together.*

"How did he die?" I had to clear my throat to get the words out.

"He broke his neck in a tumble down the stairs," the lawyer told me. "Terrible thing." He paused. "I'm relieved you remember him. I wasn't sure you would, being a distant relation."

"I've never met him." I leaned back in my chair with a sigh, ignoring Drew's inquisitive stare. "I just vaguely recall my father mentioning an Uncle Daniel when I was younger."

"I see. Well, unfortunately, Mr. Nash did not have a wife or children, and while he did will a few of his things to various members of the community, he left the bulk of his estate to be passed on to his next of kin. I'll need you to come down for the will reading on Tuesday, as well as help to execute his funeral arrangements."

Jesus.

"But I don't want an estate," I protested, a headache building between my eyes. "I'm not looking for any kind of inheritance or anything."

"Nevertheless, you're the only heir, and someone needs to take care of the funeral arrangements, so the townspeople can have some closure," the lawyer said firmly. "Unless you'd rather leave this responsibility to a total stranger?"

"No, of course not." I bit back a retort at the lawyer's pointed question, knowing he was right. I might not have known my uncle, but he was family, and I would want my next of kin to take care of my arrangements if I passed away without an heir. "Let me get my schedule cleared, and I'll come down."

I hung up the phone and then turned to Drew, who was waiting expectantly for an explanation, not even putting up a pretense of working anymore.

"So, I'm clearing your schedule?" Drew asked, raising a brow. "You do realize that you have a fashion shoot booked with Yves Saint Laurent next week?"

"Yeah, well, they're either going to have to reschedule or find someone else," I said, shoving to my feet. "I'm going to be gone for at least a week." I stalked out of the office, so I could break down my equipment and get everything in order. I had a Texas funeral to attend, and I'd never been late for anything in my damn life.

HUNTER

I WAS EXHAUSTED by the time I turned down
the road into Golden Cattle Ranch. I'd flown
back into Dallas just a few hours ago and
hopped straight into my car to make the five-
hour drive to Bramblebush, Texas. The small
town was where I'd spent much of my childhood and where Daniel Nash had lived from
the moment of his birth to the day he'd died.
I could still barely believe that had happened
over two weeks ago.

Despite my exhaustion and grief, I
couldn't help but admire the view as I eased
my custom Ford pickup down the drive.
Rows of majestic pecan trees lined either
side of the road as far as the eye could see,

disappearing over the edge of the rolling hills of my forty-acre property. I could see cattle grazing in the open fields, beyond which was a white rail fence off in the distance to my left, and as I crested the hill, I caught sight of the magnificent two-story log home that stood at the end of the road.

I parked the truck a few yards away from the white picket fence surrounding the house just as Leta, my housekeeper, came rushing down the front porch steps to meet me.

"Oh, aren't you a sight for sore eyes!" The buxom woman gave me a mile-wide smile as she enveloped me in a grandmotherly hug. Other than the gray in her dark hair and the crow's-feet branching out at the corners of her eyes, she was the exact same woman who used to fry up bacon and flapjacks for me in the mornings before school. "I'm so glad you've come to visit, Hunter. It's been awfully lonely here without you."

"Yeah, she's got no one around here to keep her company," Austin, the ranch manager and my old friend, teased as he ambled down the front porch to join us. "I guess having four ranch hands around to run the place just isn't enough for her."

Leta swatted Austin's bottom as he stepped forward to shake my hand. "Oh, don't you start!" she exclaimed, but there was a sparkle in her eye. "I give you boys plenty of attention. It's just nice to see the owner every once in a while."

"I haven't had a chance to inspect the property yet, but it looks like you boys have been doing good work around here," I said, shaking Austin's hand. I glanced over his shoulder, toward the open door of the main house. "You boys still sittin' down to lunch?"

"We're about finished, but there are probably a few leftover crumbs for you," Austin said with a smile. "Why don't you come on in? The men have been waiting to see you."

As it turned out, Leta had dished out food specifically for me, having expected me, so I dug into a hearty meal of fried chicken sandwiches and coleslaw while I caught up with the ranch hands.

When my father died, Eric, my brother, had taken over the oil side of the company while I had agreed to oversee the management of the ranches. And, with over twenty of them spread out across the state, it was a lot of work. I wanted to visit them all twice a year, but at the rate things were going, I was barely going to be able to manage once a year.

After grilling the hands about the goings-on on the ranch, I sat back and took a few moments to enjoy my food. "Has anyone been out to Old Daniel's ranch yet?" I asked. "I'm planning on going out there shortly to check on the state of things."

Austin shifted uncomfortably in his chair. "Haven't had a chance to check on things recently, but rumor has it, some new woman showed up a few days ago. A city slicker by the sounds of things."

"That so?" I sat up in my chair, frowning. "What does some city girl want with a working ranch like that?"

"Word is, she's a distant relative of Old Daniel's," Leta said as she cleared the table. "Guess she inherited the place."

"Huh. Didn't know he had any living relatives." I suddenly wished I'd kept better tabs on Daniel. I hadn't seen the old man in at least ten years, not since before I'd joined the Army in order to get away from my father's machinations and excessive need for control.

"You learn all sorts of surprising things

about people when they die." Austin pushed his chair back from the table and stood up. "We'd best get back to work now, but let us know if you need anything, Hunter."

Everyone cleared out of the kitchen so Leta could clean up. I went upstairs to grab a shower and a change of clothes. Then I headed out to the stables to saddle up a horse. I figured some riding would do me some good.

The horses had all been turned out for the day, and except for the ones the ranch hands took, they were milling about in the open pasture set aside for me. I grabbed a lead and halter from the tack stall, carefully approaching a chestnut horse that was grazing a little off to the side.

"Easy, girl."

The mare's nostrils flared as I advanced, and as she pranced, I paused, waiting for her to calm down. My inner wolf stirred from within but otherwise stayed silent. Eventually, the mare settled, and I slowly approached her, taking several minutes to soothe her, stroking her neck and muzzle.

"There you go. What's your name, sweetheart?"

"That's Misty."

I spun in the direction of Austin's voice to see him sitting astride a black gelding. "Thanks," I said. I turned back to the horse and slipped the halter and lead on to her muzzle.

"Never knew you to take so long to settle a horse before," Austin observed. "You always had such a natural touch with them, growing up."

The words were not unkind, but they rankled me anyway. "Yeah, well, I guess I lost some of my touch during my Army days."

Misty pranced nervously by my side, probably sensing my rising tension. I turned back to her, murmuring soothing words and stroking her neck. I led Misty to the stables without another word so I could get her saddled up. I knew that my body language sent a clear message to Austin that I didn't want to discuss the subject any further. He made no attempt to follow, and I sighed with relief as I saddled the chestnut.

What the hell was I supposed to tell Austin? That the reason animals fear me is because they can instinctively sense my inner wolf?

I took several deep breaths to calm myself so as not to spook the horse again. Then I saddled her up and headed out.

The first place I stopped at was the cemetery. Kneeling, I placed a bouquet of wild flowers near Daniel's headstone, surprised that only one other arrangement was there.

Has no one come to pay their respects to one of Bramblebush's oldest residents?

Anger bubbled in my gut at the idea that Daniel had died alone and friendless. It wasn't right, especially not in a community as close-knit as Bramblebush.

Leaning down, I sniffed at the other bouquet of flowers, trying to figure out who might have left them. They were beautiful, a mix of black roses and calla lilies, and as I inhaled, I caught a delightfully feminine scent, something like black cherries and vanilla. I definitely didn't recognize it as belonging to any of the girls I'd grown up with in town, and I knew no cowboy around here would smell so girlie.

Maybe it's that relative. That new girl on Daniel's ranch.

More curious than ever to find out who she was, I finished paying my respects and mounted my horse, spurring the chestnut on toward Bridle Hill Ranch. Thirty minutes later, I was crossing the cattle guard that stood beneath the open iron gate and the arch emblazoned with the name of the ranch.

Daniel's ranch was half the size of Golden Cattle, the landscape dotted with apple trees and a white clapboard house with a stable close to the center. As I rode over the acres, I frowned at the neglected state of the ranch. The grass was overgrown in several areas, indicating the cattle hadn't been moved around much, and the small section of farmland where Daniel usually grew a few crops of grain or vegetables was barren, except for the weeds that had crept across the mounds of soil.

What the hell happened here?

The ranch had been Daniel's pride and joy, and I couldn't imagine the old guy letting it all go to shit like this.

"Oh, for Christ's sake, would you come *on* already?"

The sound of a loud, angry female voice, followed by the shrill whinny of a horse, had me spurring my own horse toward the commotion. I headed around the stables toward the corral, where a tall, curvy woman dressed in skintight jeans and knee-high black boots was attempting to drag a gelding toward the stables. She swiped one hand across her face, brushing away the long wisps of curly hair that had escaped from her bun, and she looked mad as a hornet. Before I could open my mouth to protest, she yanked angrily on the rope she'd looped around the horse's neck, hurting the animal. He reared up with an angry neigh, knocking the woman over, and then dashed to the corral gate, butting angrily against it.

"Jesus!" I leaped from the chestnut and ran to the corral gate. I let myself in, resisting the desire to rush straight to the woman's aid and instead went to soothe the gelding. "It's all right, boy," I murmured, taking it slow, the way I had with Misty. In a few minutes, I had things under control, including taking care of my own horse.

I heard a groan from behind me and turned to see the woman struggling to sit up. Her top was covered in dust, and her dark hair had fallen completely free of her bun, hanging past her shoulders in thick waves.

"Are you all right?" I asked, crouching

down by her side and placing a hand beneath her back to help her up.

"Ugh." The woman pressed a hand to the side of her head. "I'm feeling a little dizzy to be honest."

"Here, let's get you to the house."

I helped her to her feet and led her to the clapboard house I'd spent many a weekend at, sitting on the porch, having iced tea with Daniel, playing cards or dice games, and listening to stories of Daniel's younger days. The house had been spotless then, maintained by Daniel and his housekeeper. But now, I could see that the porch railing and steps needed repair, and several of the clapboards had come loose, with more fixing to follow.

I led the woman into the kitchen and sat her down at the rickety wooden table, trying to ignore the state of disrepair and general neglect oozing from the house.

I grabbed a bag of ice from the freezer. "Where did you get hit?"

The woman pointed to her side.

I crouched down. "Mind if I have a look?"

"Don't see why not," the woman muttered, lifting her shirt.

I sucked in a breath at the black-and-blue bruising that was already forming along her side.

"Ouch," she hissed as I prodded gingerly at her ribs.

I tried to ignore how soft her flesh felt beneath my fingers, and I let out a sigh of relief when I felt that nothing was broken.

"You'll be hurting for a few days, but it's nothing serious," I said, pressing the makeshift ice pack to her rib cage.

She let out a gasp and then a moan, and I gritted my teeth as my blood heated. To my surprise, my wolf growled, coming to the forefront.

I like this one, he uttered.

You have got *to be fucking kidding me,* I snapped.

The woman was hurt and possibly suffering from a concussion, and my beast was having lustful thoughts about her.

Please, my wolf said, *don't pretend like this is all my fault. That hormonal surge is all you.*

"Christ," the woman remarked, holding the ice pack to her side. Her husky voice brought me out of my internal argument. "Those horses really pack a punch."

"Yeah, about that." I planted my hands on my hips and looked down at her, my anger rising. "Just what the hell did you think you were doing to that poor animal?"

"I was trying to get him back in the stable!" the woman exclaimed, her eyes flashing.

I tried not to notice how striking the color of her brown irises was against her thick black lashes and the way her sienna skin tone glowed with health.

Damn, she's stunning.

She continued, "All the other horses went easily enough. I don't understand why that one was being so damn stubborn."

I checked my wristwatch. It was barely two o'clock. "And why exactly were you trying to get the horses into the stables in the middle of the afternoon?"

The woman blinked up at me. "Well, I took them out for about an hour or so to stretch their legs, and I figured it was time to get them back inside."

I groaned, taking a seat in the opposite chair. I had a bad feeling about this. "You mean to tell me that you've been letting the horses out for only a few hours every day?"

"Well, yeah." The woman looked at me quizzically. "Why?"

I rubbed at my temples to stave off the headache I knew was coming. "It's hardly a wonder that horse was fighting you. You can't leave them cooped up in the stables all day. And why the hell were you dragging him around with that rope?"

"I couldn't figure out how to get the halter on him," the woman said stiffly. She raised her chin, straightening her shoulders despite the pain she was probably experiencing in her side. "Just who the hell do you think you are, barging in on me and asking questions like this? I sure as hell don't remember inviting you onto my property."

"*Your* property?" I countered, baiting her into giving up more information.

She lifted her chin another notch. "That's right. My name is Kia Nash, and I'm Daniel Nash's great-niece. I recently inherited this piece of property."

"And you clearly have no idea what to do with it," I muttered. Louder, I said, "Well, it's nice to make your acquaintance and all, Miss Nash, but it's obvious to me that you're in a little over your head here. I grew up with Old

Daniel, and I know if you'd met him even once, some of his love for this ranch would have rubbed off on you. It's plain you never knew the man. This ranch was his life."

Kia scowled. "Well, if that's the case, then why does it appear to be in such a shambles?"

She gestured around to the kitchen with its scuffed linoleum floors, scratched cupboard doors, and peeling, yellowed wallpaper. I couldn't help but notice that, despite the decay, every surface gleamed as though it had been freshly scrubbed.

"He left me a damn mess to clean up, and I don't have the first clue how to go about it."

I opened my mouth to berate her for speaking ill of the dead, but her eyes unfocused, and she clapped her hand to her head.

"Ugh," she said. "I really don't feel so good."

"Shit," I muttered, catching her chin in my hand so that I could look into her eyes. Her pupils were dilated. "We should get you to the doctor. Do you have a car?"

"Yeah. Why?" She blinked, trying to focus. "Don't you have one?"

"No, I rode here." I helped her to her

feet, cursing myself for my stupidity. I should have known better than to leave my truck behind. "Let's get your keys."

Her car—a beetle-green Chevy Malibu—was parked out back, and I frowned as I noticed how shiny and clean it was despite the dusty heat and the fact that it had been through such a long drive.

"My hair," Kia mumbled, touching her locks that were now a wild mass of curls. "I have to fix it."

"Oh, please." I bundled her into the car. "Trust me, no one's going to care about your hair right now."

I drove her to Dr. Miller's clinic, which was ten miles down the road and operated out of the back of his homey cottage. As I pulled up, Dr. Miller's wife came bustling out of the house, a white apron tied around her rotund figure.

"Why, Hunter Golden!" Mrs. Miller's rosy face creased into in a smile. "I can hardly believe my eyes! What are you doing here, back in these parts?"

"Just checking on the ranch," I said, taking Kia by the hand and bringing her forward. "This is Kia Nash, the new owner of Bridle Hill Ranch. She took a nasty knock to the head and banged up her ribs earlier. I'd like the doc to check her out."

"Oh, dear." Mrs. Miller clucked her tongue as she inspected Kia. "We'd better get you inside. The doctor's seeing a patient right now, but he should be done soon. Let's get you off your feet."

She settled the two of us in the parlor with tea and cookies. Then she bustled off into the back to tell her husband about our arrival. Kia's face was looking a little paler than before as she sipped her tea, but it didn't stop her from raising an eyebrow at me.

"Hunter Golden? That's quite a name you've got there."

"Thanks," I said sarcastically, raising my own cup before I took a sip of the sweet black tea Mrs. Miller had brewed.

As usual, the comment stung whenever someone brought up my family name. My father had loved money far more than his children, and it had been a bitter disappointment to him when I didn't live up to his legacy.

Kia bit her lip. "I'm sorry," she said after a moment. "I'm being an ass, aren't I?"

I laughed, the tension suddenly draining out of me. There was something about the way she bit down on her plump lower lip, those gorgeous eyes of hers downcast, that made it hard for me to be angry with her.

"You are, but considering that you've had such a rough time of it so far, I'm willing to forgive you."

She smiled, just a slight curve of her lips, but it was the first smile I had seen her give, and it softened her angular features. A surge of protectiveness swept through me, and I frowned.

What the hell am I doing, developing feelings for this woman?

She was definitely not my type, and I still hadn't figured out what her agenda here was.

Is she planning on settling down at the ranch? Or selling it?

Questions burned my lips, but I held them back. Now was not the time to ask, not when she was in pain and possibly suffering brain damage.

"Miss Nash?" Dr. Miller came out of the back room. He was an older man, dressed in a red-and-brown plaid shirt tucked into a pair of jeans, his light-brown hair liberally streaked with gray, and a pair of glasses perched on his nose. His eyes widened as he caught sight of me. "Why, hello there, my boy! It's been so long since I last laid eyes on you. Is this your lady friend here?" he asked, gesturing to Kia.

I stood up and shook Dr. Miller's hand. "Great to see you, Doc, and, no, this is not my lady friend. Her name is Kia Nash, and she's the new owner of Bridle Hill Ranch."

"Ah." The doctor's friendly gaze grew calculating. "So, you must be that mysterious relative we've been hearing about. But enough small talk," he said, helping Kia to her feet. "I can see that you're in pain. Let me take you back to the examination room."

He led her to the back, leaving me alone in the parlor with tea, cookies, and a heap of questions.

❊   4   ❊

KIA

"WELL, young lady, I must say, you're mighty lucky to escape your first encounter with a horse's hooves with only some mild bruising," Dr. Miller said as he handed me an ice pack, his examination finished. "He must have only grazed you."

Mild bruising? You've got to be fucking kidding me.

The area was dark purple and blue now, but I held my tongue about it. The doctor was right. I was lucky I hadn't broken anything.

"I guess I managed to get out of the way just enough," I said tiredly.

"Now, remember, make sure to put this

on for fifteen minutes every hour. Try lying on the couch and placing a pillow underneath your back, so you can elevate your ribs above your heart," the doctor said as he busied himself putting instruments away. He finished cleaning up and then opened the door for me. "Let's go ahead and tell your man the news."

"He's not my..." I started to say. Then I sighed.

Who am I kidding? The doctor wasn't going to listen to me.

Grumpy, I followed him out, barely refraining from stomping my boots on the floor like a child. *What has gotten into me?*

Hunter was waiting in the living room, the platter of cookies mostly demolished. He stood as we entered. I had to admit, he looked damn good in his Wrangler jeans and worn leather cowboy boots. His black Stetson was in his hands, revealing his headful of thick, wavy blond hair grown to just below his jawline. His green-and-white plaid button-up shirt was open at the collar, showcasing just a hint of the broad, tanned chest I knew must be underneath it. My fingers suddenly itched with the desire to undo a few more buttons and see if he had any chest hair to run them through.

His eyebrows rose as he caught my stare, and I felt my cheeks flush. I didn't look away though, and something like amusement glimmered in his emerald-green eyes before he turned his attention to the doctor.

"So, what's the news?" he asked.

"The news is that your lady friend suffered a good bump on the head and has some bruised ribs, but other than that, she's all right. You're going to need to check on her every few hours in the night to make sure she doesn't slip into unconsciousness. Just tap or gently shake her to wake her. If she doesn't respond, call 9-1-1 right away."

"What? I don't—" I started to protest.

Hunter cut me off. "Understood. I'll make sure she's taken care of."

"Good."

The door opened, and an elderly man hobbled in with a cane.

Dr. Miller smiled at him. "You'll have to excuse me. My next patient is here. Please see my wife about payment."

He bustled off to the older man with a jovial greeting, taking him into the back room, leaving me standing in the living room, flabbergasted.

"Shit," I muttered, patting myself down. "I don't have my purse or anything." I'd been so out of it that I didn't think to grab any of that stuff from the house.

"Don't worry about it." Hunter took me by the arm, bid Mrs. Miller adieu, and led me outside. "I took care of payment while I was waiting for you."

"You did?" I stopped dead.

Hunter tugged me by the elbow, impatient to get to the car. "Yes, I did. Can we go now? I'd like to get back to the ranch and check on those horses of yours."

"I can't allow you to pay for my medical bills," I said, digging my heels into the ground. "I did this to myself, not you or anyone else." There was no way a doctor's bill was chump change for a small-town cowboy. I didn't want to take money from someone who needed it.

"I said, don't worry about it." He tugged more firmly at my arm, and this time, I followed. "I don't want your money."

"But..."

I started to protest again, but he yanked

open the passenger side door, giving me a look that told me he was reaching the end of his patience. Biting back a scathing retort, I got into the car. I might not like his attitude, but he was helping me out. The least I could do was not give him shit about it.

We drove back to the ranch in silence. Hunter parked around the front of the house, and then he came around to help me out of the car. As I got to my feet, a sharp pain lanced through my side, and I gasped, stumbling.

Hunter instantly stepped forward to catch me, his strong hands grabbing me by the underarms. He pulled me against him, and I instinctively wrapped my arms around his torso to steady myself. Then I froze at the intimate contact. My breasts were pressed up against the bottom of his rib cage, and the heat from his hard body enveloped me, inciting an answering heat from my own.

"Are you all right?"

He tilted my chin up so that I was looking directly into his eyes, and my heart fluttered at the concern I saw in their green depths.

"Yes," I said.

My eyes latched on to the sensuous curve of his mouth, and I hastily backed away as a sudden urge to kiss him took hold. It had been a while since I'd had sex with a man, but I wasn't exactly a stranger to one-night stands. But I also knew that getting involved with this man would be a damn bad idea, especially since I didn't really know why he was here. Not to mention, I was injured and hurting like a motherfucker.

That knock on the head must have really fucked up my common sense.

"Come on. Let's get you inside." Hunter turned away, taking the porch steps two at a time.

I followed him a little more slowly and allowed him to settle me onto the cracked, faded brown leather couch.

"Just hang out here for a few and put some ice on that, okay? I'm going to go and check on the horses."

5

HUNTER

It was nearly an hour later before I stomped up the porch steps and back into the main house, and I was furious.

What the fuck has been going on at this ranch?

It had only been two weeks since Daniel died, so the sheer amount of neglect couldn't simply be attributed to my old friend's absence.

Grinding my teeth in frustration, I slammed the door behind me and then felt guilty as Kia shot up from where she'd been resting on the couch.

"What's going on?" she asked groggily, looking at me with half-lidded eyes, still clouded with sleep. Her hair was a tousled mess, and the couch had left an imprint on her right cheek from where she'd rested on it.

I was oddly touched by how damn cute she looked.

You have my permission to mate with this one, my wolf rumbled in my head.

I bit back a growl. *Fuck that.* I was not letting my wolf pick and choose whom I could mate with, for fuck's sake!

"Sorry," I muttered, scraping my shoes clean on the welcome mat inside. I joined her in the living room, sinking into the matching recliner by the fireplace. "I didn't mean to wake you...though, on the other hand, I guess I should be glad that you woke up instead of falling into an unconscious stupor. Must mean your head injury isn't so bad after all," I teased.

Kia rolled her eyes, but I caught a hint of a smile curling the corners of her lips.

She shifted into a sitting position, and her expression grew more serious as she looked at me. "Really, though, what pissed you off so much to make you slam the door?"

I sighed, taking off my hat so I could drag a hand through my hair. "It's just...I don't understand what the hell happened to this place," I said after a long moment. "I went out to check on the horses—and, by the way, I let them all out to pasture, which is what you should have done. And while I was in the stables, I decided to check on the feed stores. They're extremely low, as is the cattle feed, and with winter only a few months away, that's a really bad thing. And we need to figure out a solution for the feed since no grain crops were planted this year. I decided to go and do an overall inspection of the ranch, and there are all kinds of things that need to be fixed. Machines need to be oiled, and fences need to be repaired." I pressed the heels of my hands against my temples, a headache forming behind my eyes from just thinking about it.

"I wouldn't worry too much about any of that," Kia said, surprising me with her nonchalant tone. "I've been here for a few days, trying to figure out what to do with this place, and I'm just going to sell off the livestock and machinery, fix up what I can around the house, and then sell this place."

"Like hell you are!" I snapped.

Her plan is to dismantle the ranch and sell it off? Over my dead body!

"Excuse me?" Kia lifted her chin, her brown eyes turning hard.

I slowly got to my feet, stretching myself to my full height so that I towered over her. "You are *not* going to tear down everything Old Daniel worked so hard to keep," I told her. "That man built this whole ranch with his bare hands and passed it down to you so that it could stay in the family. Not so that you could sell it off piecemeal just to make a quick buck!"

"Well, maybe I don't want to be a rancher!" Kia jumped to her feet and then swayed slightly.

I instinctively reached out my hands to catch her, but she steadied herself on a nearby table and batted my hands away.

"Maybe it hasn't occurred to you, but I actually came from somewhere. I'm a fashion photographer, and I have my own life and plans back in New York. I'm not throwing away everything I've worked for just so I can become a rancher, which is not something I ever envisioned as a career choice, by the way."

She jabbed a finger into my chest and glared up at me. "I don't know who the hell you think you are, but you don't have the right to tell me what I can and can't do with my life!"

"A fashion photographer, huh?" I wrapped my hand around her finger, pulling it away from my chest, but I didn't let go of her hand. "Well, Little Miss High and Mighty, what if you just hired a few ranch hands to fix up and maintain the place for you, so you can go back to your glamorous lifestyle?" Something twanged in my chest at the idea of her up and leaving, and I scowled.

What the hell do I care if she goes back home? I've known her for less than twenty-four hours.

I pressed on. "Not only would you be able to get out of doing some actual hard work, but you could also even turn a profit here at the ranch and pad your wallet a bit more."

"I don't have the money to pay a bunch of cowboys to run this place." But I saw the wheels turning in her head. "You really think this place can turn a profit?"

Ah, so money is the way to this girl's heart. Good thing I have plenty of that to go around.

"Hell yeah, it can turn a profit," I said, crossing my arms. "When I was growing up,

Daniel sure was able to live nicely off what he made on the ranch while paying his hired help a decent wage."

"If that's the case, then why is this place such a wreck?" Kia demanded, sitting back down.

I followed suit.

"Where are these hired hands he was paying so well? This place doesn't look like a successful business to me. It looks like it's on its way out."

I ground my teeth. "Look, I don't know why the hell this place is such a disaster right now," I said tightly. "I fully plan on tracking down Daniel's hired help and getting to the bottom of all this. But, in the meantime, we can't just give up on this."

"I don't know the first thing about running a ranch," she said finally. "And I don't have the money to hire someone to do it for me."

"Yeah, well, I know a thing or two about ranch management," I said. "And, if I have to stay here myself for a few weeks in order to get this place up and running, I will."

Kia blinked. "Why would you do that? You've got to have other things to do."

I glared at her. "Just because I have a life and problems to worry about doesn't mean I can't make time for things that are important. Daniel was like a father to me, and I don't want to see his legacy flushed down the toilet by an ignoramus like you."

"Excuse me?" Kia nearly came out of her seat, but I beat her to it, shoving up from the battered recliner. "You fucking asshole."

"You can go ahead and act all superior if you want. But the way I see it, nothing excuses the fact that you're trying to do away with a man's entire life's work just because you're too lazy to roll up your sleeves and figure out how to make things work," I snarled. "Blood is blood, no matter how far apart you were, and it shows a lot about how much loyalty you must feel to your kin if I'm willing to put more work into whipping this place into shape than you are."

Seething, I spun on my heel and stalked to the front door.

"We're not finished talking, cowboy! Where the hell are you going?" Kia called.

"Home to get a few things. Why don't you think on what I said and let me know if anything meaningful has gone through that empty head of yours by the time I get back."

"Asshole!" she screamed.

I bounded down the steps, almost losing the battle not to shift into my beast before I hit the ground. I struggled for control and had to sit down on the ground, clutching my head for a few moments, before I was able to calm down.

There's no need to be so angry, my wolf chided when I finally regained control of my human side. *She's only trying to assert dominance over her territory.*

This isn't a pissing match, I snapped, struggling to my feet again.

Isn't it, though? You're trying to assert your dominance over her by telling her to do as you wish, and she's pushing back because she's headstrong. There was pride and a hint of smugness in my wolf's voice as he added, *That's part of the reason I like her so much. She's a challenge. It will be fun to make her submit to us.*

Jesus. I rolled my eyes. I'd had no idea that my beast was into BDSM.

No wonder the two of us didn't see eye to eye. I liked easy women who fell into my lap, not ones I had to assert my dominance over.

Yet, as I thought back to Kia, who was likely fuming over my insults, I had to admit a part of me had enjoyed the verbal sparring. She was feisty and intelligent, and she challenged me, making me want to display my superiority to her.

Shit. I've got to knock this shit off.

I walked back and forth to calm myself down, so I could go and saddle up Misty. I hadn't come here so I could bang Old Daniel's great-niece. I came here to protect Daniel's legacy, and that was all I was going to do. The sooner I got this shit over and done with, the sooner I could get back to my own damn life, away from her.

6

KIA

I looked up from my issue of *Better Homes & Gardens* as the front door swung open, and Hunter walked in. He had a pack slung over his shoulder, and his arms were full of a huge paper bag from which incredible smells were wafting.

"Wow. Well, something sure smells delicious." I got up and took the bag from him, so he could shut the door. "What is this?"

"Food. My housekeeper set some aside for me, and figuring you'd be hungry, I brought a little extra." Hunter eyed the magazine on the couch. "What have you been reading there? *Better Homes & Gardens?*"

"Oh." I shrugged self-consciously. "I just

thought I'd see if I could pick up some re-modeling tips. This house needs a lot of work."

"Hmm."

Hunter looked at me thoughtfully, and I was relieved to see there was no trace of his earlier animosity. Maybe the ride back home had done him some good.

"Well, it's a start." He took the bag back from me and headed for the dining room table. "Why don't you get some silverware?"

I fetched some plates and silverware from the kitchen cupboards and came back to find that Hunter had set out plates of country fried steak, mashed potatoes, creamed corn, and green beans.

"Holy shit, is it Thanksgiving or something?"

Hunter smiled a little. "No, we just believe in eating three square meals down here in Texas." He eyed me speculatively as he dished food onto plates for both of us. "I'm guessing it's not the same in New York?"

I shrugged. "I like to watch my weight." In truth, I was always on some diet, trying to slim down my curvy body so I could mingle with the body-shaming "it" crowd in the fashion industry. "But I guess if I were working on a ranch all day, I wouldn't need to watch my weight."

Hunter handed me a plate. "Don't see how you need to watch your weight anyhow," he said, sitting down to his own meal. "You look fine to me. Besides, most Southern men love their women with hips like honey...thick and sweet."

"Why, thank you." I wasn't sure what to make of the compliment, so I simply sat down and ate in silence for a while.

"That was delicious," I said finally, my plate practically licked clean. I didn't usually finish all my food, but the meal had been so tasty, I couldn't help myself.

Forget what I said about ranch work. Texas is definitely going to make me put on some pounds.

Hunter nodded, already halfway through seconds. "Leta's cooking is the best for miles around," he said. "I've missed eating her food."

I frowned. "I thought you said she was your housekeeper?"

He nodded. "Yes, but there's only one of her, and I own twenty ranches spread out across Texas. So, I don't get to eat from her table very often."

My jaw dropped. "You own twenty ranches?"

Hunter nodded. "My father was an ambitious man," he said, pushing his now-empty plate back. He met my gaze with a flat stare, telling me there was no pride in the statement, only an admittance of fact. "He started with the ranch up here, where Leta works now, and eventually expanded all across Texas. We're the largest provider of beef in the Lone Star State."

"Wow." I cleared my throat, suddenly feeling like an ass. "I guess that means you know a thing or two about ranching."

Hunter raised a brow. "A few things."

I sighed. "Look, I thought about what you'd said while you were gone, and I realize that...well..."

"Yes?" Hunter prompted, raising an eyebrow.

I scowled, angry with myself for feeling the need to capitulate to him. "You're right. Maybe I don't know shit about my great-uncle Daniel. I hardly even knew he existed, but it doesn't change the fact that he was family. He must have been a good person since it's clear that you loved him." I folded my arms and stared out the window, out toward the overgrown pastures faintly visible in the moonlight. *Man, there is a lot of work to do.* "But I don't want to be known as the bitch who tore down a good man's legacy just to make a quick buck."

Hunter smiled, a genuine expression of warmth softening his features. I caught my breath at the light in his gorgeous green eyes, and for a moment, I wished he was looking at me like that because he genuinely liked me.

Since when have I ever lusted after a man's approval? Especially a damn cowboy?

Though I was no celebrity, I did work among them, and I was good-looking enough that men usually chased after me with little effort on my part. Even though it had been a while, a quick fling was never far away when I needed one, and as a career-driven woman, I never wanted more than that. Yet, looking at Hunter, who somehow threw off wholesome cowboy and sexy bad boy vibes all at the same time, I suddenly felt the need to impress.

This makes it all the more important for me to get rid of him...fast.

"You know, I do appreciate your willingness to help and all, but it's going to take at least a couple of weeks to get this ranch into any kind of shape," I said, wheels turning in my mind. "And I'm sure, with twenty ranches to manage, you can't possibly have the time—"

"Are you trying to weasel out of this already?" Hunter demanded, his brows drawing together. "Because I can assure you, I have no issue with making the time for this. My ranches are fully operational and can stand to lose me for a few weeks."

"No, I'm not saying that," I said quickly, putting up my hands. "I'm just thinking... what if I try to sell the ranch off as-is to someone who really wants to use it as a working ranch and is willing to fix it up and take care of it?"

Hunter frowned. "I suppose you could try to do that...but with the state it's in right now, you'd get chump change for it. It would be much better for you to fix it up first. But I think you're underestimating just how much profit this ranch could turn for you if you kept it in good shape."

"Oh, yeah?" I folded my arms and sat back in my chair. "Well, why don't you enlighten me?"

Hunter named a figure, and my jaw dropped.

"Shit! Is that per month?"

Hunter laughed. "More like a year," he said. "But still, that kind of money is nothing to sneeze at. You could make a nice retirement nest egg...or use it for other things, I suppose." His eyes narrowed. "I gather, from your initial reaction to my proposal, you could use the money?"

I bit my lip. I wasn't exactly broke or anything...but I'd gotten into a fair amount of debt after opening up the studio and purchasing new equipment. And though I was making my payments on time, I wasn't really living frugally, so I didn't have too much in the way of savings. The ranch might not make me rich, but I could use the profits to pay back my debt and start putting money away.

"Yeah, I could use the money," I said after a moment. "But it doesn't change the fact that I have a condo and a studio waiting for me back in New York and bills to pay, all of which are going to pile up if I don't get back to work. I don't see how I can stay here long enough to get the ranch turning a profit."

"Do you have enough for a month?"

"What?" I asked.

"Do you have enough savings set aside to pay for a month's worth of expenses back home?" Hunter asked. "Because, if you do, I'm willing to make a bet with you."

"What kind of bet?" I asked, responding instinctively to the challenge in Hunter's voice. I kicked myself for displaying such eagerness in my own voice, but I couldn't help it. I had a competitive streak in me.

"Well, I bet that we can get this ranch turning a profit in one month," Hunter said. His expression was deadly serious, but there was a gleam in his eye that told me he knew he had me right where he wanted me. "I'll stay on, teach you the ropes, and help you whip everything into shape. Heck, I'll even hire some help if we need it."

"I don't want your money—" I started to say, but Hunter held up a hand.

"Think of it more as an investment," he

said. "If we pull this off, I'll get a ten percent share of the profits in exchange for my labor and experience."

"Hmm." I nodded, considering. Ten percent was more than fair, considering he was bringing a hell of a lot more to the table than I was. "Go on. What happens if the ranch doesn't turn a profit by the end of the month?"

"If the ranch doesn't turn a profit, then you can sell it off to whomever the hell you want. Another rancher, another housing developer. I won't like it, but I won't stand in your way either." Hunter raised an eyebrow. "Does that sound good enough to you?"

"Almost too good," I admitted. "I feel like I'm missing something. What's in all this for you?" I spread my hands. "In the end, no matter how all this plays out, this helps me, not you."

Hunter stood up. "I guess a tough bird like you wouldn't be able to understand something like an act of selfless love."

I shot to my feet. "And what is that supposed to mean?" I asked, gripping the edge of the table to steady myself.

Hunter laughed, but the sound was full of

mockery, all traces of his earlier warmth gone. "You're just like every other woman I've met. The only thing that lights up your eyes is dollar signs, and anytime someone does something that isn't motivated by greed or desire, you're instantly suspicious of it."

He curled his lip as he looked down at me, and though I stiffened my spine, inside, I'd never felt so small.

"Let's get you to bed, princess. The sooner you get back into fighting shape, the sooner you can get to work."

He grabbed me by the elbow and led me up the stairs, but I dug my heels in.

"Get me to bed?" I demanded. "What the hell is that supposed to mean? Aren't you going home?"

Hunter rounded on me, his big hand settling on my arm, and I gasped as I looked into his eyes. A glowing gold ring surrounded his green irises.

"The doctor said that someone needed to observe you overnight to make sure you didn't slip into a coma, so that's what I'm going to do."

"That's ridiculous," I sputtered. "I took a

nap on the couch earlier while you were gone, and I woke up just fine!"

"Maybe, but I'm not taking any chances," Hunter said, his grip tightening on my elbow. "You're not going to cop out of our agreement by going into a coma and leaving me to do all the work by myself. Now, let's go." He tugged me toward the stairs.

"Fine," I hissed. Then I yanked my arm out of his grip, stomping toward the staircase. "But I won't have you manhandling me. I'm perfectly capable of climbing the staircase, even in my weakened state," I sneered.

Even so, I had to grip the railing as I climbed the stairs to the second floor. And I couldn't help but feel Hunter's burning gaze on my ass with every step I took.

7

HUNTER

THE ALARM CLOCK on the nightstand buzzed, and I rolled over and slapped it. The digital readout told me it was two a.m., and I gazed blearily at it for a moment before remembering why I'd set it.

Time to check on Sleeping Beauty.

Swinging my legs over the bed, I tugged on the pair of lounge pants I'd packed, considered putting on the matching shirt, and then shrugged. It wasn't like she'd be able to see me very well in the dark, and I was only waking her up for a brief moment. I hoped like hell she had worn something baggy and shapeless to bed. The last thing I needed was to see her in some flimsy negligee. My cock hardened at the very thought, and I bit the inside of my cheek to counteract the lustful thoughts zipping through my mind. Thoughts I couldn't attribute entirely to my wolf.

Just don't lift the damn bedcovers.

I opened the door, and my bare feet hardly made a sound as I crossed the wooden floorboards to Kia's room at the other end of the hall. I thanked the Lord that Daniel hadn't built side-by-side—or worse, adjoining—rooms. My wolf would have wanted to take full advantage of that.

Not to interrupt your less-than-chivalrous thoughts of me, my wolf said somewhat snidely, *but something's wrong. Can't you hear it?*

I paused a few feet from Kia's door, tuning into my senses. A tiny whimper reached my ears—one I should have heard earlier, but I'd been too wrapped up in my internal battle.

"Shit," I muttered, realizing the sound was coming from Kia's room.

Is she hurt?

Maybe that blow to the ribs was worse

than I and the doctor had thought. I hoped like hell they weren't actually broken.

Pushing open the door, I stepped into the room to see Kia wrapped up in the sheets, tossing and turning. She whimpered again, a pain-filled sound, but something about it told me that it wasn't a physical pain causing the sound of distress.

"Please…" Kia cried softly. "Please, Mama…don't…" she sobbed.

My heart ached at the gut-wrenching noise. Before I could stop myself, I crossed the distance, settling myself onto the bed and gathering her in my arms.

"Shh…" I rocked her slowly, stroking her head as she trembled in my arms. Her thick locks slid sensuously along my palm, and I resisted the urge to run my hands through them. "It's okay. You're okay."

"Hunter?" She lifted her head, looking up at me through eyelashes spiked with tears.

The sheet slipped off one shoulder, exposing her sienna-hued skin, and I cursed inwardly.

Damn. She's naked.

Ignoring the sudden surge of arousal, I

looped my arm around her shoulder and pressed her head against my chest, removing her tempting mouth from my line of sight. I knew if she looked up at me like that again, I would kiss her.

"I came in to check on you," I murmured. I stroked her back, the way one might when comforting a small child, but there was nothing childlike about the smooth curve of her back, even with the sheet I'd hastily pulled back over her. "Bad dreams?"

She nodded against my chest, sucking in a deep breath. Some of the trembling subsided, and I felt a sudden surge of anger.

What the hell happened to her to make her suffer such bad dreams? And about her mother no less?

"Do you want to talk about it?"

She shook her head then slowly pulled back to look at me. Her eyes were luminous in the moonlight streaming in through the open window, and a slight breeze wafted in just then, stirring her locks.

"I want to forget," she murmured, her eyes sliding half closed as she looked at my mouth. "Please...help me forget."

"I..." I knew what she was asking for, and my body burned to satisfy her request. But my mind shouted that it was damn wrong, that I would be taking advantage of her vulnerability, and besides, I would be a fool to get involved with her. "You don't know what you're asking..."

She cut me off by pressing her lips against mine, and I froze, electricity arcing between us at the light contact. My inner wolf howled in approval, and before I knew it, my arms were around her.

"Ouch..." she breathed against my lips.

"Sorry...your injuries...we need to stop."

"Fuck that. I can deal with a little pain."

And just like that, I was kissing her. Her response was instant. She tossed the sheet off her body and climbed into my lap. She kissed me for all she was worth, drawing my tongue into her mouth and sucking with a ferocity that was surprising yet incredibly arousing.

Most of the women I bedded were fairly passive, willing to get as down and dirty as they wanted, yet always waiting for my lead. And that was generally the way I liked it. But Kia, I sensed, liked to be in control, and I suddenly realized why my inner beast was so attracted to her. He, too, wanted to rise to the challenge, to dominate her until she was drowning in him and begging shamelessly for more.

See? my wolf said smugly. *This is a real female. One actually worth chasing after, not those boring females you content yourself with pursuing. They're no challenge at all.*

I slid a hand along the curve of her hips to cup her voluptuous bare bottom, and Kia arched her back, practically purring in response. I groaned as her hardened nipples scraped against my chest. My blood burned with the desire for me to take her and learn every curve of her body like the back of my hand.

I could feel the heat of her pussy through my pants as she pressed her core against me. Her thighs clamped around my hips, and her dark hair fell around us like a curtain, creating the illusion that we were in our own little world.

"I want you inside me," she breathed huskily against my mouth, her hand reaching down between us to free my cock from my pants.

Her slender fingers wrapped around my

hard length, and I hissed as pleasure throbbed through me. It would be so easy just to slide myself into her wet folds.

No! Nothing good can possibly come of me sticking my cock inside her.

Coming is always good, my beast countered.

I had to admit, that was a pretty good argument, especially from where I was sitting right now. My balls were so tight, I thought I was going to burst if I didn't get a release soon.

Not in this case. There's a reason I don't go after women like this. I'll get attached to her, and she's going to go home to New York in a month, no matter which way this plays out. I can't afford to develop feelings for her.

I swore and then gently lifted Kia off me. I placed her bottom on the mattress before I practically vaulted off the bed like a gymnast to put distance between us.

"What the—" she protested.

"I think we've established that you're awake now," I interrupted. I couldn't afford for her to get enough steam to make any kind of argument because I knew I would crumble and begin fucking her like a soldier on leave. "Good night."

I closed the door and headed for the hall bathroom, remembering there was a bottle of lotion sitting on the counter. I sure as hell was going to need it if I planned on getting any more sleep tonight.

8

KIA

WHEN THE SUN finally rose the next morning, I had hardly gotten a wink of sleep. I just wanted to pull the covers over my head and hide from the world. I was utterly mortified about the way I'd so wantonly thrown myself at Hunter last night, especially when all he'd been trying to do was help me out of my nightmare. Now, with the way I'd rubbed myself so shamelessly against him, he probably thought I was some kind of sex-crazed hussy.

My cheeks burned as I remembered the way he'd jumped out of bed, as though he couldn't get away from me fast enough. I supposed I would have reacted the same way if someone had tried to jump my bones out of the blue like that.

But no one forced him to grab my ass last night. And he sure sounded like he liked it when I squeezed his cock...which was pretty damn big. There were stronger women than I who would cream in their panties just to have even a fraction of that inside them.

I scowled because, typically, I wasn't one of those women. This was part of the reason I was so embarrassed about my total loss of self-control last night.

It must have been that damn bump on the head.

It had fucked with me, which explained my brazen reaction, as well as why I'd been seeing things yesterday when I looked into his eyes.

As for his initial reaction to my advance... well, he *was* a man. He'd have to be dead not to respond in some way when a naked woman draped herself all over him, especially when that woman looked like me. I knew men liked my tight, curvy figure and thought I had a pretty face. Usually, that was the only reason men needed to fuck. But Hunter had clearly come to his senses before we went all the way, and the truth was, I should be thankful. I didn't need to get involved with a man I'd be leaving in a matter of weeks.

Yes, that's right. I should be thankful. Not offended that he'd tossed me on my ass like a hot potato and practically sprinted out of the room like a track star.

Yes. I am fucking thankful.

The aroma of frying bacon wafted through the crack in the door to tease my nostrils, and my stomach rumbled.

Better go and face the music. Grumpily, I tossed the sheets off me. I rummaged through the closet for a serviceable pair of jeans and a T-shirt that I wouldn't mind getting dirty. Then I stomped my way to the bathroom to take a long, cold shower.

We're going to be working together for the next month, so we'd better set some clear boundaries.

❧ *9* ❧

HUNTER

T HE FAINT CREAK of the floorboards above told me that Kia was up, and I bit back a groan. I'd been hoping that she'd sleep in because of her head injury and that I'd be gone by the time she woke up.

Guess it's a good thing I made enough breakfast for two.

I flipped the bacon on the griddle.

A few minutes passed before Kia came down the stairs, looking absolutely stunning, and the way she fit in her blue jeans...

Hell. There damn sure ain't no curves like hers on the back roads in Bramblebush.

I scowled. Kia was nothing but temptation, and now I found myself wishing she had stayed in her room to rest and heal. I really didn't need her help to get the ranch into working order. I had plenty of money to hire help if I needed it. But the other part of me was relieved she'd made it through the night. I hadn't dared go back into the room to check on her again, and I'd felt guilty about leaving her alone the rest of the night. But there was no way I would be able to resist her advances again, especially since my inner wolf was so eager to fuck her. The bastard had berated me endlessly for walking away from her.

Gathering up the platters of scrambled eggs and bacon to bring to the table, I turned to see Kia hovering in the doorway, uncertainty written all over her face. Her cheeks flushed as I met her eyes, and with some satisfaction, I noticed the dark circles under her eyes.

She didn't get any sleep either.

"Sleep well?" she finally asked huskily.

"Yep."

I'd jerked off three times last night, and it still hadn't been enough. My body continued to burn with the need to be inside her and only her, which frustrated me to no end. I'd tried to imagine perfect, busty blondes while I was pleasuring myself, but I had been unable to get off until I pictured Kia straddling me, her mouth crushing mine as her breasts brushed against my chest. Her bust was smaller than I usually liked—a C-cup at best, I gauged—but she more than made up for it in the ass department. The feel of her sexy ass in my hand...

Biting back a curse, I ripped my attention from my lustful fantasies and stalked toward Kia. Her eyes widened, and she backed up through the doorway, no doubt thinking I was going to do something to her, but I brushed straight past her to the dining room table and started setting the food out.

"Why don't you help set the table?" I asked calmly, as though I weren't trying to beat back fantasies of bending her over the dining room table, grabbing a handful of her hair, yanking her head back, and fucking her until we both went blind.

"Yes, of course," Kia said quickly. She fled back into the kitchen.

It took a little longer than was probably necessary for her to fetch plates and forks, but that was okay with me. I needed the time to compose myself as well. By the time she came back in, I was almost completely calm again.

We ate in silence for a while, the only sounds in the room the clink of silverware against plates, the crunch of bacon between teeth...and Kia's heartbeat, I realized, cursing my heightened senses. It sped and slowed intermittently, like a roller coaster, and it was putting me on edge.

"Why don't you spit out whatever it is you're thinking?" I said flatly, picking up another slice of bacon with my bare fingers. "I can tell you're nervous about something."

"I'm not nervous," she snapped, but she didn't meet my eyes. "I..." She took a breath and then looked up at me. "I just wanted to apologize for last night. It was a mistake, and it won't happen again."

What the fuck? It was a mistake?

I should have been relieved. I'd been thinking much the same thing, but internally, I flinched, the words more painful than they had any right to be.

"Don't worry about it," I told her. Then I took a bite of my bacon and chewed. "I know you weren't thinking straight. You probably thought I was someone else."

"Yeah, sure."

We both knew it wasn't true, but Kia seemed relieved that I was giving her an out.

Her shoulders relaxed. "So, um, what's the agenda for today?"

"Not much," I admitted, pushing back my empty plate. "I'm going to be gone most of the day, and you shouldn't be doing any hard labor, not while you're recovering, and especially not while I'm not around to make sure you don't nearly kill yourself again."

Kia raised her chin. "I survived before you got here."

I rolled my eyes. "Yeah, and God only knows how the hell you managed that. No, you need to take it easy and rest up today," I told her firmly.

"But we only have a month," Kia protested. "I can't just sit around here doing nothing. Surely, there's something I can do while you're gone."

"Oh, I wouldn't worry about that," I said, tossing her a shit-eating grin. I stood up and cleared my plate from the table. "I'm definitely going to be putting you through your paces to-morrow, so I suggest you take full advantage of your rest day while you still can because you'll be cursing me to hell and back tomorrow." I turned away, heading for the kitchen again.

"Yeah, right," Kia said, belligerence in every syllable. "I'm no stranger to hard work."

I didn't answer, and when I came back through the door, a scowl marred her pretty face.

"Where are you going?" she called as I headed for the front door.

I turned back to her for a moment, my expression dead serious now. "I'm going to find the sorry souls who used to work for Old Daniel and make them tell me what the hell happened here." I couldn't believe that they hadn't had some kind of hand in the ranch's decline, and I was going to get to the bottom of this mess today.

A foul mood settling in from the lack of sleep, sexual frustration, and the task that awaited me, I climbed into my truck and drove off, looking forward to giving someone a good ass-kicking.

10

KIA

I PEEKED through the living room curtains as I watched Hunter get into his truck and drive off. I waited until the truck reached the end of the road and disappeared through the gate before I rushed out the door and over to the shed near the chicken coop in the backyard I had noticed a few days ago but had yet to investigate.

To hell with what Hunter had said about taking a rest day. I was feeling a lot better and perfectly healthy—aside from a case of sleep-deprivation, and that was nothing new to me. As a fashion photographer with tight deadlines, I'd spent many a late night slaving away in my darkroom, developing film either for my clients or for my own personal projects. Just because I wasn't a rancher didn't mean I wasn't a hard worker. I was an independent woman, for God's sake, and I didn't need a man to tell me what to do.

It took me a few tries to get the shed door open and a trip back to the house to grab a broom and beat away some of the cobwebs that had formed in the doorway. But finally, I made it inside, and to my delight, I found the cans of paint and stain I was looking for. I had to make three trips to grab everything I needed, but eventually, I was standing in the living room with buckets, rollers, brushes, and cans littered all around the front door.

I spent a few minutes sorting out all the colors, deciding what I wanted where, and then I rolled up my sleeves, preparing to move the furniture out of the living room. While I knew I would be a fool to attempt to do anything out in the fields or stables without Hunter, I was no stranger to interior design, and I was determined to prove to Hunter that I could get something done without a man around.

Taking a deep breath, I grabbed the dolly I'd found in the shed, dusted it off, and got to work.

11

HUNTER

M**Y FIRST STOP** was Lucy's on Main, the only diner in Bramblebush and the town watering hole during the day. I ordered a cup of coffee and a doughnut. Then I proceeded to ask around about Daniel and who had been working on the ranch before he had passed away.

The Bramblebush townsfolk were always friendly. They were happy to see me after I'd been away so long, but their cheery smiles disappeared pretty quickly when I started asking about Daniel. They told me that, as the rancher had gotten older, he'd started going crazy. Got real paranoid, they said, as if someone was out to get him. He'd fired all his ranch hands except one and cut his housekeeper's days down to once a week, claiming he couldn't trust anyone to be around him anymore. I managed to get the name of the housekeeper and the ranch hand and left the diner, troubled by what I'd heard.

Did Daniel really go crazy?

I got back into my truck and drove away. It certainly sounded as if he had lost it.

Why, in his right mind, would he have fired all his staff and let his ranch go downhill? Simply because he had been paranoid that one of them might hurt him?

Or was it more that Daniel had been paranoid he might hurt them? Had he sent them away for their own safety?

I could understand that. For a long time, I'd been afraid to go near my ranches or spend much time with anyone for fear that my wolf beast would take over, and I'd hurt someone. But the two of us had formed a harmonious relationship—sex life notwithstanding—over time, to the point that I could even approach and handle animals that were instinctively afraid of my darker half.

What had happened to Daniel to make him drive his own employees away? I doubted it had been something as drastic as turning into a hybrid wolf-shifter, but I did think Daniel had been in some kind of danger.

It hurt my heart to think that my old friend had acted out of irrational fear and insanity and ended up destroying the ranch he'd worked so hard to build. No, more than likely, Daniel had had a good reason for what he did. And I was determined to find out what it was.

It took me several minutes to locate the dirt road that led to the housekeeper's cottage, located on the outskirts of town. By that time, dark clouds were starting to gather on the horizon, signaling an impending storm. The woman's name was Carla Jones, and I remembered her from my childhood— a sunny blonde and mother of two, who always had a kind word for everyone. She'd been Old Daniel's housekeeper when I was a child, and I guessed she'd never moved on from the job.

Parking the car out front, I noticed that the house was small, probably no more than one bedroom, but meticulously maintained, the paint on the shutters and eaves new, and the window boxes bursting with brilliant flowers. No one came out to greet me, but I saw the green lace curtains shift slightly, and I knew from the small Ford pickup parked nearby that someone was home.

Taking off my Stetson, I approached the door and knocked politely. "Mrs. Jones?" I called. "It's Hunter Golden. Do you mind if I call on you for a few minutes?"

The door opened, and Carla looked out at me through the screen door. Her blonde hair had faded to silver sometime in the last twenty years, and she had laugh lines around her eyes and mouth, but there was a haggard look about her and a watchfulness to her dark eyes that I didn't remember.

"Hunter Golden," she said slowly. Then a smile lit her face, softening some of the starkness of her features. "Oh, I remember you! You were that nice boy who always came out to keep Mr. Nash company and help him out on the ranch." Her face fell a little at the reminder of her former employer, strengthening my suspicions that she knew something. "What can I do for you?"

"Well, see, Mrs. Jones, that's just the thing." I clutched the brim of my hat in both hands, trying to come off as contrite and as unassuming as possible, no small feat at six foot two and two twenty. "I've been over at Old Daniel's ranch, trying to straighten things out after his death, and I've noticed some mighty strange things. I was hoping to talk to you to see if you could help clear up a few things for me."

"Oh, I don't know." Mrs. Jones pressed her lips together, casting her gaze away from me. "I'm sure you've gotten plenty of information from the townsfolk already."

"Yes, but I'd like to ask you anyway and see if I can uncover a few more details."

"I really don't think I have anything new to tell you," Mrs. Jones started to say. Then, she jumped as a clap of thunder shook the sky.

"Please, won't you at least let me in for a cup of coffee?" I pleaded, grinning inwardly at the perfect excuse. "I'd hate to be caught up in the storm that's coming. It's bound to be a doozy." I leaned around her a little bit, sniffing the air. "Is that your peach cobbler I smell? You always did make the best in town."

"Oh, all right," she relented, smiling a little. There was nothing like appealing to a woman's vanity to get what you wanted. "You can wait the storm out in my parlor for a few minutes."

She stepped aside to let me in and waited until I wiped my boots on the mat before taking my coat. "Why don't you have a seat?" she said, pointing to the green velour love seat situated next to a matching recliner and couch, all arranged around a glass coffee table. "I'll go fetch you a nice slice of cobbler."

I glanced at the bright, floral-patterned carpet as Mrs. Jones quickly escaped into the kitchen, and I wiped my boots again before sitting down. I looked around at the cream-colored wallpaper and still life paintings that decorated the walls and paused to admire some of the knickknacks littering the brass mantel above the fireplace. Everything was clean and neat and in its proper place, which I imagined made sense, as Mrs. Jones undoubtedly had little else to do but clean, bake, and rearrange the furnishings.

She came back with the cobbler she had reheated and a mug of steaming black coffee. "Sugar and creamer are right here," she told me, gesturing to the two small silver containers on the coffee table.

"Thank you." I ignored both the sugar and creamer and sipped the strong black coffee, which was piping hot. Not wanting to lay right into her and scare her off, I took a bite of cobbler, closing my eyes and savoring the dessert. "Just as good as I remember," I said, smiling.

"Why, thank you." Mrs. Jones beamed with pride. "I win a prize for it every year at the County Fair."

"I'll just bet you do."

Rain started tapping on the roof, lightly at first and then turning into a stronger staccato. We made small talk for a few minutes, and I learned that her husband had passed away a few years ago, and her children had both moved out of state, searching for more lucrative pastures.

The rain was coming down in earnest now, drumming incessantly on the rooftop and drenching the lawn outside.

"So," I said when my plate and mug were both empty, "tell me about what went on with Daniel these last couple of years."

Mrs. Jones glanced toward the window, and I raised an eyebrow. There was no way anyone was out there, eavesdropping in this downpour.

"What is it that you're so afraid of?"

"I'm not afraid of anything," Mrs. Jones said defensively. "There's nothing to be afraid of. Mr. Nash was just getting senile in his old age. He was probably on some kind of medication that caused his paranoia, and that was why he fired so many of us. I don't know what else there is to say about it."

"I'm sorry, but I just can't believe that," I said gently but firmly. "The Daniel I knew never would have let the ranch go to hell. It was his pride and joy. And I know he wouldn't have willingly put so many people out of work. There has to be some kind of reason beyond that."

The former housekeeper sighed. "Well, I did notice that Mr. Nash got awfully tightfisted," she told me. "He started getting on my case about buying less food or cheaper cuts of meat when I went to town, and I noticed he would wait until the last possible moment on a lot of fencing repairs. Johnny Heller, the only ranch hand he kept on, begged him to increase his hours, so he could do more work on the ranch, but Mr. Nash wouldn't hear of it. He worked his fingers to the bone, trying to make up for the loss of three hands, but he couldn't keep up, and things started going downhill real fast."

"So, he was having money problems," I mused. I chewed on this piece of information for a few moments. "Do you have any idea why? Was there anything that happened before he started firing his workers?"

Mrs. Jones glanced to the window again before answering, "I really can't say that there was—or at least, not right around the time he started getting so tightfisted," she said, her voice dropping down to barely above a whisper.

I frowned. *Who the hell does she think is listening?*

"But about a year before it happened, a man came to the ranch, trying to get Mr. Nash to sell."

"Sell? You mean, the ranch?" My jaw dropped. "Old Daniel never would have done something like that."

Mrs. Jones pressed her lips together. "You'd be right about that," she said tightly. "He refused to sell. Took up his shotgun and damn near chased the man off his property when he wouldn't let up. Served him right too. It's not polite to badger a man so." Her face fell a little. "But sometimes, I wish he'd just given in."

"Why?" My eyes narrowed. "You think this man had something to do with why Daniel was having money issues?"

"I can't say for sure," Mrs. Jones said. "But before Daniel started letting go of his workers, he spent an awful lot of time poring over his books. He'd spend half the night up in his study, raking over the numbers, and he never would tell me what was going on." She wrung her hands. "I just can't help but think that man had something to do with it."

I frowned. It was a long shot, I had to admit, but it was the best lead I had so far. "Do you remember anything about the man? His name, what he looked like, where he was from?"

Mrs. Jones bit her lip. "I'm not right sure. I think his name was Branson or Branford or something like that. He was tall with dark hair and dressed in a nice suit. Had a Texas accent, but it was a watered-down version, as if he'd been living up north for too long." She wrinkled her nose. "Certainly didn't have much of any of our manners."

I bit back a smile. Mrs. Jones was a Texan woman through and through. "Well, that's certainly a start," I said. "Mrs. Jones, can I ask you something?"

"Yes?"

"Why do you keep looking at the window? Do you see or hear something out there that I'm missing?"

"Well, no...not exactly." But Mrs. Jones started wringing her hands again. "It's just that I can't help but think Mr. Nash's death wasn't an accident."

I frowned. "What do you mean?"

"Well, they say he fell down the stairs when he died, but I can't imagine how that happened. Mr. Nash might have been getting old, and certainly, he was working himself hard, but he was still strong and mostly healthy. It just doesn't seem like him to take a tumble down the stairs." She glanced out the window again.

"I see." I wasn't quite so sure that she was being silly. "So, you're thinking that someone might have murdered Daniel and that they could come after you next?"

Mrs. Jones let out a nervous laugh, waving me off as though I were being ridiculous. "I'm probably just being silly," she said. "There's been no proof of foul play, and I didn't see anyone at the ranch that night."

"But, nevertheless, you're afraid." I leaned forward and looked the old woman in the eye. "Look, Mrs. Jones, I'd like you to come back to work at Bridle Hill."

Mrs. Jones blinked. "You want to hire me back on as the housekeeper?" she said, her eyes wide. "You didn't tell me you'd bought the ranch."

"I didn't," I said. "But I am helping the new owner get it back into shape."

"New owner?" Mrs. Jones wrinkled her nose. "Did some outsider buy the place or something? I hope it wasn't that man," she said with a shudder. "I'd hate for him to have finally gotten what he wanted this way."

"No," I said with a slight smile, "Daniel left the ranch to his next of kin, who happens to be a young woman from New York."

"A New Yorker?" Mrs. Jones laughed. "And she wants to keep the ranch?"

I shrugged. "I convinced her to give it a try," I answered. "Just trying to honor

Daniel's wishes to keep it in the family. We have a little arrangement going, and there's a lot of work to do. We sure could use some help with the house. And, in case you really are in danger, I'd feel a lot better if you stayed with us on the ranch instead of out here, by your lonesome."

Mrs. Jones nodded. "It certainly would be nice to have some extra money," she said. "I was barely squeezing by between my social security and the little bit Daniel was still paying me. And since he died, I've been worried I'd have to sell the house and move in with one of my children." Her lower lip trembled a little, and then she squared her jaw. "But I'm afraid I'll need to think on it for a night, Mr. Golden. I can't go making rash decisions, not at my age."

"I understand completely." I looked out the window and then stood up. "Well, it looks like the rain's let up enough for me to drive home safely. But I do hope you'll say yes, and at the very least, I'd love it if you came by to see the ranch sometime."

"Oh, I will," Mrs. Jones said. She surprised me with one of her old sunny smiles. "I'd love to meet this new relative of Daniel's to see if she bears any kind of resemblance to him."

"Well, she sure has his mouth," I told her. I was struck by just how hot it made me even to think about Kia's mouth. I'd nearly lost my mind when she kissed me last night, and thinking about it made my lust come roaring back. "She's feisty, so I have a feeling you'd probably like her."

I took my leave of Mrs. Jones, thanking her for her hospitality before I climbed into the truck.

I mused on what I'd said to her, realizing I was sincere. Mrs. Jones probably would like Kia. Even though Kia was a pain in the ass, she had a certain amount of spunk to her that the old woman would find charming. I could easily imagine Mrs. Jones plying Kia with heaps of food and regaling her with all kinds of stories of the farm, and I was suddenly eager to make it happen. Maybe Kia would develop an affinity for the ranch and her deceased great-uncle if she knew more about him and would decide not to sell the ranch.

Maybe she'll even decide to stay on the ranch, my wolf suggested.

I scoffed. *Trade in her glamorous New York City lifestyle to put down her roots in Texas? I don't fucking think so.*

But the idea did have some appeal, and I found myself whistling a happy tune as I drove away, heading over to pay Johnny a visit.

12

KIA

"Whew!" I wiped the sweat off my brow as I finally moved the last of the furniture back into place. I'd managed to do not only the living room, but also the dining area in the four hours since Hunter had been gone, and I felt pretty proud of myself.

A few coats of paint, and the place looks ten times better already. Just wait until Hunter sees it!

My excitement was much the same as a child's would be when they finished a project and counted down the minutes until they could show their parents, but I felt no shame in it.

Everyone wants approval every once in a while, don't they?

Humming to myself, I washed off the brushes, gathering up the first set of supplies to take back to the shed. I stepped outside, pausing on the porch to take a breath of clean, rain-scented air. The cloud cover had finally broken, revealing a gorgeous sunset that painted the sky in hues of red, purple, and orange, and there was even a rainbow arcing through the sky.

Maybe ranch life isn't so bad.

The sound of an engine prevented me from examining that outlandish thought any further, and I looked up to see a shiny black sedan rolling through the gates. Frowning, I carefully placed my armload of supplies onto one of the porch chairs. Then I stood at the top of the steps and waited to see who the unexpected visitor was. Anxiety squeezed my stomach, and I wrapped a hand around one of the roof support pillars, holding on for support.

Don't be silly. I'm sure it's just one of the towns-folk coming to scope out the new owner.

I'd already had a few visitors before Hunter showed up. But none of them had driven a nice car like this, and certainly, none of them wore thousand-dollar suits, I noted as the man got out of the car.

Shit. Why didn't I go back into the house for my gun?

Well, at least he doesn't look like he's armed.

I didn't see any bulges in his suit jacket indicating that he was carrying. But he was a tall, solidly built guy who probably out-weighed me by at least sixty pounds.

And there are no neighbors to hear me if I scream. Damn...I am pretty much a sitting duck. Fuck ranch life.

"Why, hello there!" the man greeted me, waving to me from his car.

He started walking in my direction, and I gripped the post more tightly, wondering if I should go back into the house. Something about this man was setting off all of my alarm bells. But he stopped at the bottom of the porch steps, maintaining a reasonably safe distance, so I stayed where I was.

"Miss Kia Nash, I presume?" he asked, a hint of Texas in his accent.

"Who's asking?"

He smiled, revealing rows of perfect white teeth, and I had to admit, he was hand-some with his swarthy complexion and perfectly styled dark hair. But the smile didn't reach his cold, gray eyes.

"My name is Samuel Bradley," he said. "I'm a real estate developer, and I heard that Mr. Nash, the former owner, recently passed away." His smile dimmed a little. "I was planning on buying the ranch, as one of my associates had told me it was going up for sale, but then I found out you'd inherited it." He hesitated. "Would you mind if we went inside and talked for a moment?"

"Yes, I do mind."

The last thing I wanted to do was invite this strange man into my house. But part of me was interested in what he had to say. After all, he was clearly interested in buying the ranch. But the other part of me knew it would be wrong to renege on the bet I'd made with Hunter. Besides, I'd already decided to honor my great-uncle by not selling the ranch to a housing developer.

"I'd feel more comfortable with talking on the porch."

"Well, I just thought it would be nicer to go inside since it's all wet out here," Samuel started to say as a truck rolled in through the gates.

He turned to look, and I was relieved to see it was Hunter's truck.

"Friend of yours?" Samuel asked mildly.

"Yes, actually," I said before smiling. "He's assisting me with renovating the ranch."

"I'm willing to offer you a hundred thousand for it," Samuel said quickly, turning back to face me. "Instantly wired to your account as soon as you sign the papers."

My jaw dropped. "A hundred thousand dollars?"

"Hey!" Hunter slammed his cab door behind him before jogging up to us from his truck. A thunderous scowl marred his handsome face as he looked back and forth between Samuel and me. "Who the hell is this guy?"

I knew it was wrong, but Hunter's aggressive tone got my back up, and I responded in kind. "His name is Samuel Bradley," I said sweetly, "and he's offering me one hundred thousand dollars for the ranch."

Hunter raised an eyebrow. "That's a mighty nice sum," he told Samuel. "Wonder why some bigwig like you would pay so much money for a run-down place like this."

"This is prime real estate here," Samuel

answered, flashing Hunter a sharklike smile that made me remember I probably shouldn't be on Samuel's side. "Not that it's any of your business."

"Well, I hate to break it to you, buddy, but it is my business." Hunter planted himself directly in front of Samuel, putting a buffer between Samuel and me that I was grateful for. "This little lady is sticking around for a bit."

"Is that right?" Samuel asked, looking over Hunter's head to raise his brows at me.

I nodded. "Hunter is the one who agreed to help me fix up the ranch."

"Is that so?" Samuel's expression seemed mild, but there was a cold gleam in his eye that told me he wasn't pleased by this news. "Well, best of luck to you." He stepped smoothly around Hunter, produced a card from his inside jacket pocket, and handed it to me. "But in case you change your mind and are interested in selling me the ranch, here's my card. I hope you'll be in touch."

Samuel sauntered back to his car, as if he hadn't a care in the world, and I let out a sigh of relief. We watched as he turned his car around and drove away, and the knot of tension in my stomach eased as the black sedan crossed the cattle guard and moved out of sight. That was, until Hunter rounded on me with a look so deadly, I knew I'd have been struck dead on the spot if looks could actually kill.

"I wonder," he said quietly, "if you would have made the deal with that guy if I'd come back but five minutes later."

"Of course not," I said hotly. "Why would you even say such a thing?"

"Because I saw the dollar signs in your eyes," he spat, closing the space between us until we were barely three inches apart.

I felt his breath on my face, and a tremor of fear went through me as I noticed that the gold rim was back in his eyes.

So, I didn't imagine it. That is some weird birth defect.

"You wanted to make that deal so bad, you could practically feel the money in your hot little hands," he finished.

"And so what if I did?" I shot back, rising onto my tiptoes so I was nose-to-nose with him. I was *not* going to let him intimidate me, freaky eyes or otherwise. "It doesn't make me any less of a person just because I faced temptation today. What should matter to you is that I. Didn't. Give. In. To. It." I jabbed my finger into his chest with each word to make my point, which was a little like trying to poke a boulder. His chest was a wall of solid muscle.

I suddenly remembered what those rock-hard pecs had felt like when I'd pressed myself against them, and I had to take a moment to shove the memory from my mind. "I don't know what kind of bug got up your ass today, but you can get off your high fucking horse anytime now," I snarled. "I haven't given you any reason to think that I'm untrustworthy, so fuck you if you think you can go ahead and be my judge, jury, and executioner."

Turning on my heel, I stomped back inside the house, slamming the door.

13

HUNTER

I STARTED AFTER KIA, intent on giving her a piece of my mind.

How dare she talk to me like that!

I was her fucking lifeline, and it was time she started treating me like one. But I paused at the sight of a bunch of paint cans and brushes, piled on the porch chair closest to the door.

"What the..." I muttered, picking up one of the brushes and thumbing the bristles. The horsehair was still slightly damp, indicating recent use. "Did she actually use these today?"

Carefully, I opened the front door and stepped inside. Then I stared at the living room in shock. Gone was the mottled white paint, replaced by a lovely shade of lemon yellow that I knew would really brighten the room during the day. She'd also repainted the baseboards and molding a bright white, and upon closer inspection, I couldn't see a single brushstroke out of place.

I noticed how smooth the walls were. *She even used primer.*

Glancing back toward the entrance, I saw another pile of painting supplies and knew she'd done more than just the living room. Guilt swamped me as I realized, while I'd been out investigating, she'd been here, at home, doing manual labor. And instead of complimenting her on it, I'd laid into her about something she hadn't even really done.

God, I'm such an asshole.

Not willing to face Kia quite yet, I quietly gathered up the painting supplies and returned them to the shed in the backyard. I stood out there in the twilight for a long moment, thinking about everything that had gone on today before finally heading back inside.

Closing the front door behind me, I heard the microwave running in the kitchen.

I walked in to find Kia standing in front of the machine, staring intently at it, as if it were the most fascinating thing in existence.

"I was going to paint the kitchen too, but I didn't have time," she said coldly without turning around. Her back was stiffer than a steel pole in the dead of winter. "Sorry I'm such a fucking disappointment."

"Oh, Kia," I sighed, feeling like ten kinds of asshole.

I crossed the distance between us, turning her around by the shoulders. Her eyes were hard and brittle, as if they might crack at any moment and tears would spill forth.

"I'm sorry. It was wrong of me to snap at you like that, and I know you didn't do anything to deserve it. I was just in a really bad mood when I got here, and when I saw you with that man..." My mood darkened as I thought about that slimeball. "Well, I overreacted, and for that, I apologize."

Kia's shoulders relaxed a little, but the look in her eyes didn't soften. "Well, okay then." The microwave beeped, and she turned around to take her food out.

I eyed the frozen dinner with distaste.

"You don't need to eat that crap, Kia," I protested. "Leta's coming by with dinner at any moment."

Kia shook her head. "It's fine. I'm not even very hungry anyway. You can help yourself to the food when it gets here."

She took her microwaved dinner into the dining room, and I followed her. I paused to admire the pale gray paint she'd chosen for the walls.

"You did such an excellent job," I told her, awed.

Kia blinked, clearly surprised at the compliment. "You really think so?" she asked hesitantly.

"Absolutely." I pulled out a chair and sat beside her, determined to repair the rift between us. We needed to be able to work together if we were going to get the ranch in shape. It wasn't as though I actually cared about her feelings otherwise. "Where did you learn to paint so well?"

Kia smiled a little, and some of the anxiety in my gut eased.

"My college roommate was going to school for interior design, and she was constantly *upgrading* our dorm room," she said, her eyes shining fondly with the memory. "At first, it was annoying. But eventually, I looked forward to her redesign projects and even helped her with some of them. I learned a lot from her."

"Well, from what I can see here, she was a pretty good teacher," I said, looking at the walls again. "Are you two still friends?"

Kia nodded, but her face fell a little. "She moved to the West Coast for a job though, so I haven't seen her in years. We try to keep in touch."

The doorbell rang, and I excused myself to answer the door. "Leta!" I exclaimed, my stomach grumbling at the bags of food in her hands. I reached down to take them from her and then stepped back to let her inside. "I was just daydreaming about sinking my teeth into a rack of your delicious baby back ribs."

"Well, you're in luck, honey, because that's what I made tonight." Leta took one of the bags back from me before I could protest, and then she bustled past me and into the kitchen. "Ooh, Lordy, someone did a nice job with the paint in here!" she said, looking around. Her eyes settled on Kia, who had stood up from the table, and Leta smiled. "You must be Miss Nash."

"Please, call me Kia," she answered as Leta set the bag on the table. Kia came around to give Leta a handshake, squeaking when the old woman roped her into a hug. "It's nice to meet you," Kia choked out.

"Nice to meet you too," Leta replied before releasing her to give Kia a critical eye. She then reached out and pinched Kia's waist, causing her to squeak again. "You've got a real nice figure, but I'd feel a lot better if you put a bit more meat on your bones, Miss Nash. Let's see if we can do something about it."

Bemused, I set the other bag on the table and watched as Leta unpacked containers of macaroni and cheese, ribs, creamed spinach, and large, round biscuits that made my mouth water just looking at them. Even Kia looked ravenous as she came back from the kitchen with a stack of plates and silverware. Leta's cooking had that effect on people.

"I do hope I brought enough," Leta said as she served us both. "You two look famished." She folded up the paper bags, tucking them under her arm, and then she picked up her purse and prepared to leave.

"You're not staying?" Kia asked around a mouthful of biscuit.

"Oh no," Leta said. "I've still got more work to do back at Golden Cattle Ranch before I turn in for the night." She leaned in and kissed me on the cheek. "You two be good now."

I walked Leta to the door, making sure she made it to her car safely. Generally, there was no danger out in these parts, but coyotes and wolves sometimes crossed onto ranch property, and I was still feeling edgy after that strange man's visit today. I needed to talk to Kia about what I'd found out and make her understand just what it was we were up against.

When I returned to the dining room, I found Kia scooping a second helping of ribs and macaroni and cheese onto her empty plate.

"I thought you weren't hungry," I teased, settling back down to my own plate of food.

"It's amazing what a compliment and the sight of good food can do for one's appetite," Kia said dryly, but there was a twinkle in her eye. Her frozen dinner had been shoved off to the side, practically untouched. She paused for a moment. "I appreciate your apology, Hunter. Some guys don't have what it takes to admit they're wrong."

I snorted. "I can't say I don't struggle with that issue every once in a while," I admitted, "but I don't want there to be any bad blood between us. But, really, Kia, I found out some important stuff today that you need to know about."

Between bites of food, I told her about my visit with Mrs. Jones and Johnny. Kia interrupted occasionally to ask a question, but for the most part, she listened in silence, a look of intense concentration on her face.

"Did the ranch hand corroborate her story?" she asked.

I nodded. "Johnny pretty much said the same thing—that Old Daniel had fired off most of his workers, drastically cut down on Johnny's own hours, and became extremely tightfisted about money."

"I don't know what the hell was going on," Johnny had said, scowling off into the distance. "I thought maybe Mr. Nash had lost a bunch of money on an investment or a wager, but I can't see why

he'd have risked the ranch on something foolish like that. The only thing I can think of is that he was being blackmailed, but I can't think of what someone would have over a sweet old guy like him."

"Do you know who that slicker works for?"

Kia frowned. "Um...hang on a sec." She dug a card out of one of the front pocket of her jeans. "Samuel Bradley," she read. "President of Bradley and Radcliffe, Inc."

I scowled. "Mrs. Jones said she thought the man who'd tried to buy the ranch off Old Daniel might've been Branson or Branford. It's too much of a coincidence."

Kia sat back, her plate practically licked clean. "You think Samuel was the same man who tried to buy the ranch from my great-uncle?"

"It's a strong possibility," I answered. "Mrs. Jones said the man seemed pretty insistent about buying the ranch, so I can't imagine him not coming back out of the woodwork once he discovered Old Daniel had died." I frowned again. "You know, I can't help but think I've heard the name Bradley and Radcliffe somewhere," I mused aloud. "I think I'll call up my brother in the morning and see if he knows anything about the company."

"That sounds like a good idea." Kia stood up and started clearing the table. "I think it would be best to see what you can find out about this guy before we make any kind of decision. I'd hate for us to go after a man who's innocent."

I snorted. "Trust me, I've done business with men like Bradley. He's far from innocent."

The man's reptilian gaze sent shivers down my spine.

Samuel Bradley was stone-cold, no doubt about it. The kind of guy who would do whatever it took to get what he wanted. I could easily imagine him blackmailing an old man in an attempt to force him to sell off the ranch.

Putting aside the subject for the night, I helped Kia clear the table. Then I took up a position in front of the farm sink and started filling it with water. "I'll wash," I said, tossing Kia a dishrag. "You dry."

We worked in silence for a long while—me scrubbing plates and setting them in the dish rack, Kia hand-drying them and putting them away. She was fast, I observed. I picked up my own pace to try to keep up with her. She was drying the dishes faster than I could hand them to her.

"You used to do this for a living or something?" I asked, half joking.

Kia's answer surprised me. "I had a dishwashing job at the college cafeteria," she told me without pausing from her work. "Between that and the freelance photography work that I did later on in my college career, I was able to afford my books and my share of room and board at the dorm."

I frowned. "Didn't your parents help you out with any of that?"

Kia shook her head. "No. When my father left my mother for another woman, he cut me out of his life too. And, well...my mother wasn't good for much of anything, except a bottle of whiskey." She spoke matter-of-factly, but I knew she had to be hurting about it still. "I worked my ass off in high school, so I could earn an academic scholarship to NYU. I got my undergrad degree in photography and imaging, and I haven't looked back since."

"Wow." I pulled the plug, allowing the sudsy water to drain out of the sink. "Well, your mother must have at least been proud of you, right?"

"Honestly?" Kia hung the dish towel on the hook over the sink. "I don't think she even noticed I was gone. She's dead now—cirrhosis of the liver, I was told—so I'll never be able to know for sure."

She shrugged, and I was suddenly overwhelmed by a fierce need to take her in my arms, tell her that her mother was wrong and that she was amazing and didn't deserve to be neglected, but her eyes were flat. I knew instinctively that she wouldn't welcome my pity. She was a self-made woman, and she wanted to be acknowledged for what she was now, not where she'd come from.

"Maybe you could show me your photography sometime," I suggested after a moment.

Kia smiled a little. "Maybe. I didn't bring my portfolio or anything, but I have taken a few shots with my DSLR since I got here, and I'll show them to you if I ever get a chance to develop them."

"I'd like that," I said. And I really meant it.

I was filled with a burning curiosity to find out more about this woman, about her passions and what made her tick. We stood there, smiling at each other for a long moment, and I felt something subtle shift in the air between us.

"I'd better get to bed," Kia said quietly, breaking the spell.

"Yeah," I said softly. This time, when the memory of her naked body rose in my mind, I didn't try to fight it or push it away. "We've got a long day tomorrow."

I watched as she walked away, heading up the stairs to bed, and waited until I was sure she was behind the closed door before turning in.

14

HUNTER

THE NEXT WEEK passed fairly quickly. I showed Kia how to muck out the stalls, clean tack, and feed and care for the horses. I spent an afternoon teaching her how to saddle and mount a horse and then ride one, and though she was nervous at first, she ended up taking to it like a duck to water. Once I was confident she could hold her own reasonably well, I took her with me on fence inspections, and we worked on the repairs together whenever we found them.

I also hired Johnny to come and help me herd the cattle to a different pasture and told the former ranch hand I'd hire him at least once a week to help with the task. The man was grateful for the opportunity, meager though it was, and I determined, once I was done here, I would convince Kia to hire Johnny back on to his old job as ranch hand.

Mrs. Jones also came to visit, declaring that she liked the looks of things so much that she would come back on as the house-keeper. Her cooking wasn't quite as good as Leta's, but it was still delicious, and Kia and I looked forward to her home-cooked break-fasts, lunches, and dinners.

No longer worried about keeping the house clean or keeping up with the dishes, Kia somehow managed to dredge up the energy to work on home improvement projects during the evening, and though I would have much rather kicked back with a beer, I helped her out. I knew there was something soothing to her about working on the interior design projects, and besides, the house did need to get done.

By the end of the week, the ranch was looking a hell of a lot better. The horses were well cared for, the house was coming together, and the fences and even some of the machinery had been repaired.

"It's finally time for me to start training

those horses," I told Kia over dinner on Sunday night.

Mrs. Jones had made us steak, potatoes, and glazed carrots, the latter of which Kia seemed to be particularly relishing.

"Training them?" she asked, popping another carrot into her mouth. "What for? They don't seem like they need to be broken in or anything."

I laughed. "I forgot that you don't know how Daniel made the majority of his money. He trained stock and cutting horses, selling them to cattle ranchers."

"Cutting horses?" Kia frowned. "What are those?"

"They're horses specially trained to separate a cow from the herd," I explained. "Cutting horses are used in competition, while stock horses are used around the ranch to help herd cattle."

"Huh. I guess I never thought about it, but it makes sense that you'd need horses specifically trained for that," Kia mused. "And you know how to train cutting horses?"

I nodded. "It's been a while, and I'm not as good as Daniel was, but he taught me the ropes. Some of these horses are already a fair way into their training from what Johnny told me, so I should have a few ready to sell by the end of the month."

"That would be very exciting," Mrs. Jones said as she came to clear some of the plates away. "It would do my heart good to see this ranch starting to turn a profit again. And I wager the townspeople would be happy too."

The phone rang then, and Mrs. Jones started toward the living room to pick it up. "I wonder who on earth that could be."

"I'll get it." I stood up and placed a hand on Mrs. Jones's arm, already having a good idea of who it was. "You go ahead and finish what you were doing."

Excusing myself, I went to the living room and picked up the phone resting on the side table next to the couch. "Bridle Hill Ranch," I said, settling myself into the chair.

"Hey, Hunter," Eric greeted me. "How are things going?"

"Pretty good." I gave him a brief overview of what Kia and I had accomplished that week. "I'm pretty hopeful we can get this ranch back on its feet by the end of the month. In the beginning, I was worried Kia might end up being dead weight, but she's really been holding her own."

"That's great," Eric said. "Really good to hear. Listen, I got your message about that guy from Bradley and Radcliffe shaking Kia down about the ranch, and you're right—they're bad news. They pounce on ranches that are down on their luck, buy them up, and turn them into housing developments."

"I knew it," I hissed. My grip tightened on the phone, and I forced my hand to relax before I cracked the phone. Then I thought about what Eric had said and paused. "Wait, you said ranches down on their luck? But, from what I understand, Old Daniel's ranch was going strong when he was approached to sell."

"Well, maybe the guy who approached Daniel wasn't the same guy who approached the two of you last week," Eric suggested. "It follows the pattern that Bradley would approach Kia now, when the ranch is declining. I don't see why he would have made an offer on the ranch when it was still functional. It would have cost him a hell of a lot more to buy it then than it would now."

"What you're saying makes sense," I said,

"except that Bradley offered Kia one hundred grand for the ranch, which is easily five times what it's worth right now."

"One hundred thousand!" Eric exclaimed. "That's crazy!" There was silence for a moment. "He has to have an ulterior motive," Eric said finally. "There's some kind of strategic advantage Bradley will gain by buying that ranch, and I think it's worth finding out what that is."

"I don't suppose there's any chance you might be able to help me on that end?" I asked. "I'm not very good with business."

Eric sighed. "I'll see what I can do, but I can't make any promises. I'm pretty busy these days. I'll let you know if I do find anything. But in the meantime, I suggest you do your own research."

"Will do. Thanks, brother." I hung up the phone and then stared into the empty grate of the fireplace for a long while, thinking on what my brother had said.

Is it possible that the man who approached Daniel a few years ago is completely unrelated to Bradley?

I supposed it was, but that didn't mean I believed it for a second. And, even if it was,

Bradley was still up to something, and I was determined to find out what it was.

The sound of a floorboard creaking caught my attention, and I looked up to see Kia standing in the doorway, gazing at me. She was freshly showered, both of us having cleaned up before dinner, and her damp hair gleamed softly in the lamplight. As usual, I was struck by the urge to take her into my arms, to kiss those luscious lips, and to run my hands through her hair, but I refrained, just as I had countless times in the past week.

"Mrs. Jones said to tell you good night, and she took off to her cottage," Kia said, stepping into the room. She paused for a few seconds. "I overheard some of your conversation." She perched herself on the edge of the couch, a small smile on her face. "You really think I'm doing a good job?"

I grinned. "You're doing a fantastic job, darling," I told her, reaching out and taking her hand in mine. That proved to be a mistake as a spark of electricity arced between us, and her pulse fluttered in her throat, but I tried to ignore it. "I couldn't have asked for a better ranch hand."

Kia affected a playful, haughty look. "I'll have you know, I'm the owner of this ranch," she said, looking down her nose at me. "And I don't appreciate you referring to me as a ranch hand."

"Yes, ma'am," I said.

We both laughed. I began rubbing my thumb across her hand, circling the sensitive spot between her thumb and forefinger, and silence fell over us. I heard Kia's breath catch in her throat, and I bit back a growl as I caught the scent of her intoxicatingly delicious arousal.

I should let go of her hand now.

My entire field of vision narrowed until Kia was all I could see. All I could think about. And I knew I was close to breaking.

"Hunter," Kia whispered.

And that was all the invitation I needed. Growling, I pressed her back against the couch, kissing her deeply. Kia kissed me back, hesitantly at first and then with more ardor as I drew her into a passionate embrace. My cock hardened, already throbbing with the need to be inside her, and when she whimpered with pleasure, I knew I was lost.

To hell with my requirements.

I slid my hands beneath her black tank top. I was going to take her to bed tonight. Without breaking the kiss, I hauled her into my arms and wrapped her legs around my waist. Then I carried her up the stairs. I stumbled a few times, causing her to squeal, but she didn't let go of me or stop kissing me, and eventually, we made it to my room at the end of the hall.

I kicked the door shut behind me. Then I turned on the lamp and laid her out on the bed. "I want to see you," I said huskily. "Every fucking inch of your beautiful body."

Eyes dark with desire, Kia sat up and ever-so-slowly removed her tank top, exposing her torso inch by inch. I watched silently as she revealed her breasts, which were covered by a black bra, and I had to remind myself to be patient and not rip the offending garment away. She made a show of tossing the tank top aside. Then she reached around leisurely and popped the front clasp on her bra, letting it glide off her shoulders.

"Damn..." I groaned as Kia took one breast in each hand and began massaging the round globes.

How could I ever have thought they were too small?

They were perfectly round and perky with chocolate-hued nipples I desperately wanted to nibble and taste.

"More."

"More?" Kia raised an eyebrow, a flirtatious smile playing on her sensuous lips. She moved one hand down her abdomen and then popped the top button on her jeans. She slipped her hand beneath the waistband of her panties. "Mmm," she moaned as she touched herself, her eyes drifting closed as she leaned back against the pillows.

Unable to take it anymore, I grabbed her zipper and yanked it down. Then I ripped off her jeans and panties in one fluid motion. Kia let out a shocked cry as I settled myself on the bed. She looked at me with wide eyes as I spread her legs.

"Enough with the teasing," I growled. "It's my turn to play."

❧ 15 ❧

KIA

I TREMBLED as I looked into Hunter's eyes. There was no denying the gold glow in his irises as he looked at me as though he was ready to devour me, but it was excitement rather than fear that coursed through my veins. I knew this was a bad idea, that having sex with Hunter could never be something as simple as a quick fuck, but I was too far gone to care.

"Your pussy looks so good," he whispered, staring down at my shaved mound. He licked the pad of his thumb and then reverently slid it across my folds, sending a spark of pleasure into my core. "But I want you wetter than this."

He slid two fingers inside me, and I moaned as he stretched me, sending more of those delightful sparks skipping through my nerve channels. My back arched involuntarily as he began to massage my clit with his finger, circling slowly while thrusting his fingers in and out.

"Oh God," I gasped as his fingers found my G-spot. "Yes, right there." I let my head fall back against the pillows, closing my eyes as the sensations built gradually. I savored each pulse and throb. I'd never really been big on foreplay before, preferring the feel of a big, hard cock inside me to a man's fingers or mouth, but for some reason, Hunter was able to find my sweetest spots.

"Open your eyes," he demanded, his voice low and rough and so sexy I didn't even think about the fact that he was ordering me to do something. "I want you to look at me when you come."

I opened my eyes, and Hunter lowered his head, replacing his thumb on my clit with his tongue. Instantly, my whole body stiffened, and I grabbed his head, pressing him close, craving more.

"Yes. Please, don't stop," I gasped.

I looked down at him then, and the sight of him between my legs was so hot, I came harder than I ever had in my life. Waves of pleasure poured out from my center. The waves started to ebb, and I thought it was over. But he kept licking me, and another surge of bliss crashed down on me again and again until I was begging for mercy.

"Holy shit," I panted, collapsing against the sheets. "That was fucking amazing."

Hunter lifted his head, a self-satisfied grin plastered on his face. His jewel-toned eyes smoldered with lust, and I thought I would melt into a puddle right then and there.

"It sure did sound pretty good from where I'm lying." He crawled up my body, hemming me in with his hands and knees on either side of me. "You taste really good," he murmured, lowering his lips to mine. "I could eat your pussy all damn day."

Our lips were about to touch when a shrill scream pierced the night. Hunter and I both jumped, and then he vaulted off the bed and ran over to the window.

"What the hell is going on out there?" I demanded, reaching for my jeans at the foot of the bed. My heart was racing again, and this time, it had nothing to do with the man in the room.

"It's one of the horses!" Hunter shouted, dashing from the room. The next thing he said made my heart drop into my stomach. "They're being attacked!"

16

HUNTER

I GRABBED a shotgun from the rack by the door and rushed outside, heading for the stables at a dead run. The horse was still screaming, and the others were stomping and neighing in fright. I was confusing the sounds, but beneath all of the equestrian racket, my sensitive ears picked up on the noise of growls and teeth ripping into flesh.

Something's out there for sure.

I pumped the shotgun and then fired a warning blast in the air. The horse screamed again, and then it was silent before I heard a scampering of paws against dirt. I caught a glimpse of a large creature with shaggy fur dart from the stables before disappearing and running off into the night. The predator in me wanted to chase after the intruder, but the more rational part of me knew I needed to check on the horses.

Grabbing the lantern hanging outside the stable doors, I paused to light it and then held it aloft while cautiously entering the stables. Most of the horses were still in their stalls, stomping nervously, banging against the doors, their terrified whines and snorts putting my beast on edge. I wanted to stop and soothe them, but the stall door at the end was open, and I slowly crept toward it to investigate.

What I found inside made me wince in sympathy. Inside was a roan mare named Twilight, lying on her side and covered in bleeding bite marks and gashes. The ones on her forelegs were deep enough that I could see a hint of bone, and one of those legs was at an odd angle, bone poking through the skin.

"Oh, Twi," I murmured softly, crouching down to stroke the horse's mane.

The mare let out what could only be categorized as a whimper, but she seemed to settle down as I caressed her.

"You were so close to finishing your training too. I'm sorry."

I aimed the shotgun at the horse's head and then paused as I heard a rush of footsteps outside. My nose told me it was Kia, and a second later, she dashed to my side, bundled up in a robe over her jeans, her face concerned and hair flying every which way.

"Oh my God," she gasped as she caught sight of Twilight. "What happened to that poor horse? And...what are you doing?" Her eyes narrowed on the shotgun in my hand.

I sighed, lowering the weapon so as not to cause her further alarm. "I have to put her out of her misery," I explained, reaching out and stroking Twilight's matted hair.

The horse quivered beneath my palm, and my heart ached for her.

"What?" Kia looked horrified. "You... can't just kill that poor animal! How do you know she won't recover from her injuries? I'm going to call the vet, see if I can get someone down here."

She started to turn away, but I reached out and lightly squeezed her by the ankle.

"Kia," I said, my voice low, "first off, calm down and stop yelling. You're agitating the horses." I waited until she stilled. "Second of all, come here. I want to show you something."

Reluctantly, Kia lowered herself into the hay and dirt so that she was kneeling next to the horse and me. I took her hand and placed it on the horse's left foreleg.

"Do you see anything odd about this?"

Kia was silent for a long moment. "It's broken," she finally said in a small voice.

"Yes." I took a breath. "Even if Twilight manages to survive her other injuries, which is doubtful at this point," I said, gesturing to the large quantities of blood matting the hay beneath the mare, "this leg will never heal properly. It isn't just a matter of her being lame. She'll literally never be able to put any weight on it, and with the amount of mass she has, it just isn't feasible for her to try to hobble around on three legs. She'd live out the rest of her life in constant pain and misery."

Tears filled Kia's eyes. "But..."

I laid my hand over Kia's. "I'm sorry, sweetheart. It has to be done."

Nodding, Kia rose to her feet and fled the stables. I sighed. Then, resigning myself to the task, I pumped the shotgun, aiming at the horse's head, then fired.

~

"I HAVE TO SAY, THIS IS THE STRANGEST thing I've ever seen," Dr. Kensington said as he knelt down in the bloody hay and examined the dead animal in the stall. "A horse being attacked in its own stall. Never heard of such a thing in my entire career, and I've been doing this for thirty years."

I stood just outside the stall, watching the vet bend his salt-and-pepper head over Twilight's body as he scrutinized her injuries.

"What do you think did this?" I asked.

We were completely alone in the stall. I'd let the horses out before I turned in last night so they wouldn't have to be around the stench of death, and Kia was still in bed.

"Well, the bites and claw marks are certainly canine in nature," Dr. Kensington said, "but the jaw length is far too large for a dog or coyote. My best guess would be that it was a wolf...but even then, it would have had to be a huge one." The vet shook his head, finished his examination, and stood up. "I hate to say it, but you did the right thing by ending Twilight's life. She never would have recovered from that broken leg."

"Appreciate it, Doc." I took out my wallet to pay the man and then helped him to his car. I stood on the porch, watching the vet drive off, thinking long and hard about what the doctor had told me and what my own senses had informed me when I did a little of my own investigation last night.

My first impression when I'd seen the beast running out of the stable was that it was a wolf. But I'd discarded the theory on my second impression, which was based on the animal's size. Once I'd let the horses out and I was alone in the stables, I'd picked up on what I thought was the scent of a wolf, though it was slightly off from what I remembered wolves smelling like.

The doctor had told me that the bites were canine, but they were too large to be a dog or coyote or really even a wolf. But I had smelled something like a wolf and seen something like a wolf, and I could only draw one conclusion from all of this. The beast that had attacked Twilight was a wolf-shifter.

But what the hell was a wolf-shifter doing

running around in rural Texas and killing off horses?

I could understand if a rogue or nomadic shifter had decided to take down a cow or sheep for some food while passing through, but the shifter had left the cattle untouched despite the fact that they were much easier targets. The idea that the animal that had attacked Twilight was a shifter also explained why the stall door was open, I realized. The stall door hadn't been damaged in any way, so I couldn't see how an animal could have gotten it open.

Shaking my head, I went back inside the house. Then I called Johnny and a few other guys in town to come and help me remove the dead horse from the stable and get it to the butcher. After the emotionally and physically draining tasks were completed, I returned to the house ready to tackle the rest of my to-do items for the day. Upon entering the house, the delicious aroma of bacon and griddle cakes hit me, and I followed the scent into the dining room, only to see Kia sitting at the table, picking at a plate of eggs and griddle cakes. She was bundled up in a bathrobe and looked a little worse for the wear, her hair hanging wildly around her face, with dark circles beneath her red-rimmed eyes.

"Hey," I said softly, sitting in the chair next to her. I put my arm around her. "Are you okay?" I knew it was a dumb question as she clearly wasn't, but I couldn't think of anything else to say.

A lone tear slipped from the corner of her right eye, and she angrily swiped at it, as though she couldn't bear for me to see her tears. "It's stupid," she choked out, her voice barely a whisper. "I hardly knew any of the horses. I've only been taking care of them for a week. Yet..."

"You grieve," I finished for her. I squeezed her shoulder gently. "There's no shame in that. Twilight was a good horse, and you learned to ride on her, so it's only natural that you would feel her loss."

"I overheard you on the phone," Kia said suddenly, lifting her head to glare balefully at me. "Don't take Twilight to the butcher. I want to give her a proper burial."

I nodded, silently acquiescing to her request. There was no point in explaining to her that selling Twilight to the butcher would allow us to recoup some of the monetary loss from the horse's death. Kia was in no state to think about business.

"We'll bury her this afternoon."

Johnny and the other men arrived, and we spent the rest of the morning hauling Twilight's body out to the burial ground that Kia had picked out and then digging a hole large enough to bury the animal. I tried to get Kia to go back inside, but she refused, planting herself next to the horse's body, her knees drawn up to her chest as she watched the men work. Her brown eyes were vacant, as if she were far off in another time and place. I couldn't help but wonder what she was thinking about. I didn't press her though, sensing she wanted to be left alone.

Storm clouds slowly gathered on the horizon as we worked, and by the time the grave was finished, thunder and lightning were crackling through the sky. Mrs. Jones came out with umbrellas for everyone, and we all huddled around the grave as Johnny officiated the ceremony. Everyone said a few nice words about Twilight, even the ranchers who had never met her before, and then we buried her, placing flowers atop the grave.

Kia quietly thanked everyone and then disappeared into the house before I could say anything.

"Leave her be," Mrs. Jones said when I attempted to go after her. "I have a feeling she's grieving for more than just a dead horse."

Nodding, I paid the men for their help, and then Johnny and I saddled up and herded the cattle to another pasture.

Just a few more weeks of this, and the pastures will be looking right as rain. Although that won't matter if I end up losing the bet.

That's the most defeatist thing I've ever heard you think, my inner beast growled. *So, we lost one horse. That doesn't mean we're going to lose another. We're just going to have to work a little harder to make up for the loss.*

Easy for you to say, I grumbled.

But my wolf's words actually made me feel a bit better. The truth was that I still had three weeks, and a lot could happen in that amount of time.

Still, that wolf-shifter I smelled was pretty alarming, I told my beast. *I hope he was just passing through and that he'll leave the horses alone.*

My wolf snorted. *If you're going to trust in things like hope and faith, you might as well throw in the towel now.*

Right.

I needed to be on my guard. The horses were the ranch's most valuable commodity, and since we only had ten right now, we couldn't afford to lose another. Until I knew that the wolf wasn't going to come back, I was going to have to make sure the horses were guarded. And since I couldn't bring myself to put any of the other men in that kind of danger—they were only human, after all, and I wanted them to stay that way—it meant I'd have to do it myself.

17

KIA

When I finally awoke, the sun had set below the horizon, leaving only a few faint streaks of color in the sky as evidence that it had ever been there.

Twilight, I mused groggily.

And the reminder of the horse nearly threatened to send me into a spill of tears again. But I held them back. There was no way I was going to cry any more today. My head felt as though it had swollen to the size of a watermelon, and my eyes and nose ached from all the crying I'd already done.

God. I rolled onto my back and stared up at the ceiling. *Hunter probably thinks I've lost my damn mind.*

I bet no woman he had ever met lost her head like this over a horse she'd barely known. If he told the story to any of my friends or acquaintances in New York, they would never believe it.

Kia, getting emotional over an animal? That woman wouldn't even be moved to tears by the TV commercials with Sarah McLachlan singing "Angel."

I owed Hunter an explanation for my behavior, and I was going to give it to him before I chickened out, hiding behind my mental walls again.

Dragging myself from the bed, I shuffled into the bathroom and splashed some water on my face. I attacked my bedraggled locks with a brush for a few minutes, and then, knowing I wasn't going to look any better unless I started caking on makeup, I left the bathroom and made my way down the hall to Hunter's room.

No one answered when I knocked, and a quick peek inside the room revealed nothing but rumpled bedsheets. I flushed as I remembered that I had helped rumple those sheets, and desire warmed my blood despite my shitty mood, surprising me. I shouldn't even be thinking about sex right now, yet the way his hands and mouth had felt on me, teasing my most private places—

Shaking my head, I closed the door and headed downstairs. I found Mrs. Jones cleaning up in the kitchen after dinner, but no Hunter or any of the other ranch hands who had been here to help out today.

"Where is everyone?"

Mrs. Jones glanced over her shoulder toward me and then set down the dish she was holding. She briskly dried her hands on a towel. "Oh, you're looking much better, sweetheart," she said, taking my face between her hands and peering into my eyes. "But you look like you could use a bite. Let me heat you up some leftovers."

I shook my head. "I'm not hungry right now. I just want to know where Hunter is."

"That foolish man?" Mrs. Jones clucked her tongue disapprovingly as she opened the fridge door, clearly ignoring me as she pulled out what looked like fried catfish, baked sweet potatoes, and steamed vegetables. "He's outside, sleeping with the horses. Says he's waiting for the animal that attacked poor Twilight to come back. I told him he was crazy to put himself in danger like that, but he won't hear of it."

A lump formed in my throat at the thought of Hunter being so dedicated that he would sleep with the horses, and I scowled at the emotional response. I'd probably raged and cried on this ranch more than I had my entire life, and I wasn't sure how I felt about that. Either Texas ranch life was getting me in touch with my emotional side, or it was driving me batshit crazy.

"I'm going to go out and check on him."

"Hang on, sweetie." Mrs. Jones caught me by the wrist as I was turning away. "Let me finish heating this food up for you."

"But I'm not—"

"Maybe you're not hungry, but I can guarantee you, Hunter will happily eat all of this and wonder why you didn't bring seconds. That boy is insatiable when it comes to food." Mrs. Jones took the container out of the microwave and then handed it to me along with a fork wrapped in a napkin. "Go ahead, honey. I'll just finish up here and head off to bed."

I took the food out to the stables, my ears straining to hear any kind of unusual activity, but there was nothing but the sound of chirping crickets and the occasional rustle in the grass. Brilliant stars littered the night sky, and the moon was round and nearly full, providing a gorgeous luminescence to the evening. It was like nothing I'd ever seen in NYC. The light pollution generally blotted out all but the brightest stars in the sky, and even then, they were faint pinpricks. Here, I could actually imagine them as the enormous, gaseous balls of fire they really were, providing light from trillions of miles away.

It made me realize that my place in the world, in comparison, was so very, very small. Pushing that thought aside for later, I approached the stables. I wondered if anyone was actually inside since there was no light coming from the structure, but I figured maybe Hunter didn't want to alert the animal to his presence if it came back. I shook my head, agreeing with Mrs. Jones. This was foolishness. Surely, there was a better way to ensure the safety of the horses.

"Kia?" Hunter's voice called as I stepped inside, a husky whisper in the darkness, sending a shiver of desire through me. "Is that you?"

"Yes." I squinted through the shadows, trying to figure out Hunter's location. "Where are you?"

"Third stall on the left."

I found the stall in question, which was wide open, and as my eyes adjusted more fully to the darkness, I could make out Hunter lying on his back in a pile of hay. "That can't be comfortable," I told him, settling next to him on my knees, the container of food still in my hands.

"It's all right," Hunter said, sitting up and taking the Tupperware. "But I have to say, it's become a lot more comfortable now that I have some pleasant company." He gave me a roguish smile that made my heart flutter like a schoolgirl's. "I'm talking about the food, of course," he added as he removed the lid from the container. "Ow!" he cried as I smacked him on the arm.

"Serves you right," I said with a sniff, folding my arms.

Hunter took a bite of his food, and my stomach rumbled, my body apparently relaxed enough to want food again. Raising an eyebrow, Hunter scooped up another bite of catfish and then offered it to me.

I shook my head. "No, I'm fine. I'm sure you're hungry."

He eyed me skeptically. "When was the last time you ate?"

I shifted uncomfortably beneath his stare. "I might have managed a few bites of breakfast."

Hunter rolled his eyes. "Eat some of this before you keel over and die."

He shoved the piece of catfish between my lips before I could protest. An instant burst of flavor made me completely forget about anything but my hunger. Snatching the Tupperware from Hunter, I devoured almost two-thirds of the meal before finally handing it back to him.

"Sorry," I said sheepishly.

Hunter patted me on the back. "That's my girl. I bet Mrs. Jones heated up this food for you anyway, didn't she?" he teased.

I nodded, and we lapsed into a comfortable silence as Hunter finished off the rest of the meal.

"You're looking a lot better," he said quietly, hooking an arm around my shoulders and drawing me against him. "Did you sleep well?"

"You could say that." I'd slept heavily, dreamlessly which I was grateful for. "I want to explain myself to you."

"You don't owe me any explanations," Hunter said, rubbing my shoulder in a gentle rotation that soothed me. "Everyone has their moments sometimes, and I don't fault you for wanting to give Twilight a good burial."

"Yes, but you don't understand," I protested. "When we buried Twilight today... well, I wasn't totally burying Twilight."

Hunter was silent for a moment. "Then who were we burying?"

I let out a long sigh. "When I told you my mom died of cirrhosis of the liver...well, I lied," I said, my shoulders sagging a little. "Not that she wouldn't have died from that eventually or from overdosing on heroin or something, but that isn't what happened."

"How did she die, then?" I could hear the frown in Hunter's voice as he tried to figure out where I was going with this.

"She was attacked," I whispered, my body trembling slightly as the memory of that horrible night took shape in my eyes. "I came home to check on her one night, and she was in her room with...a man." I shuddered. "She often brought men home, usually for sex in exchange for a quick fix, but something wasn't right this time. I heard screams and someone snarling, and I opened the door to find..."

"To find what?"

I laughed nervously. "You're probably going to think I'm crazy. The police and my neighbors all thought I was crazy too."

"Try me."

"Well, the only way I can describe him is as some kind of monster," I said. "Like a wolf-man or something. He had coarse, thick hair all over his body and bloody fangs that looked as though they could bite clear through my arm." I shuddered again. "For a moment, I thought he was going to attack me too...but he just turned and leaped straight through the window, shattering the glass. When I looked over the side of the sill, I could see him running away in the distance even though it was a two-story drop. I called 9-1-1, and even though my mother's body was covered in claw and bite marks, they didn't believe me when I told them what I saw," I whispered. "Shit. Most of the time, I don't believe it myself. So, I put it behind me, went back to college, finished my degree, and started working." I shook my head, consumed with self-loathing. "I didn't even arrange a funeral for my mother. She was cremated by the state. They offered me the ashes, but I refused them. God only knows where they ended up."

"Oh, baby." Hunter dropped a kiss on the top of my head and rubbed my back. "I don't think anyone would blame you for that, not after the way your mother treated you."

"My grandparents did," I said, my voice hollow. "I'd never met them in all my life because they wanted nothing to do with me... their out of wedlock grandchild. You see, her parents were deeply rooted and involved in the church. Her father was a pastor and her mother the church clerk. So, they disowned my mother for being unmarried and pregnant, but a month after her death, they came out of the woodwork, scolding and blaming me for what had happened to their daughter. They read about her death from the obituary in the paper and demanded to know why they hadn't been told or informed about any funeral or anything." I smirked a little. "I might have said a few unkind things to them in return."

"That's unbelievable." Hunter's voice was dark with anger, and I looked at him in surprise to see a thunderous scowl on his face. His expression softened a little when he saw me staring. "You deserved better than that, darling."

A lump formed in my throat in response to the compassion in Hunter's voice, and I turned away before I started tearing up. "I don't know," I said slowly. "I've never believed that people deserve anything other than what they make for themselves in life, and I've worked hard to live up to that ideal. But I guess I must have felt guilty in the back of my mind, about not honoring my mother's death, because when I saw Twilight, covered in those scratches and bites...it reminded me of my mother, and I just lost it." I took a deep breath then, and as I let it out, I felt some of the weight on my heart dissipate. "I guess, when we buried Twilight, I was really burying my mother."

Hunter nodded. "Mrs. Jones thought as much, though she didn't specifically say anything about your mom. She just said she figured you were probably grieving about more than just Twilight.”

I smiled a little. “She’s a wise woman.”

“Yes, she is.” We sat in silence for a moment, simply enjoying each other’s presence, before Hunter spoke again, “You know, I’ve never met a woman like you before.”

I arched a brow. “You mean, a crazy person?”

Hunter laughed. “Oh no, I’ve met plenty of those. I mean someone as fiercely independent as you,” he said, smiling down at me. “Or as hardworking.”

I shrugged, uncomfortable with the praise even though the battered part of me wanted to soak it all up. “There are other women out there who are more successful than I am.”

“Maybe. But how many of them would have dropped everything they were doing to come down here and take care of a ranch owned by an uncle they’d never met? You probably could have just hired a Realtor to sell this place off to the highest bidder without ever setting foot on the property,” he told me, his expression serious now. “But instead, you showed up to see the place with your own two eyes, and you got your hands dirty even though you had no idea what the hell you were doing." He laughed again. "That might have been fool-headed of you, but it's still admirable."

I finally smiled. I couldn't help it. "Well, that might be the closest thing you've given me to an apology for yelling at me that day."

Hunter kissed my forehead. "I am sorry," he whispered against my skin, "for giving you such a hard time in general. You've risen to every challenge I've given you so far, which is saying something, considering there are women in this town who would turn up their nose if you asked them to do so much as clean out a stall. You're more woman than any woman I've ever met...and, believe you me, I've met quite a few of them."

I opened my mouth to make some kind of snarky retort, but Hunter suddenly reached up to stroke my cheek, his touch featherlight and tender.

There is so much... I wondered, gazing into his eyes. *Is it lust? Love? Compassion?*

I didn't know, but whatever it was, the emotion dragged me under his spell, drawing me closer to him until our lips were a breath apart.

"Kiss me," Hunter whispered, gazing at me with half-lidded eyes.

I did, pressing my lips against the sensuous curve of his mouth. I kissed him with soft strokes of my mouth against his at first and then grew bolder with tiny nibbles and the sucking of his bottom lip. Hunter groaned in response and then dragged me onto his lap, sliding his hands up the back of my shirt. Adrenaline rushed straight to my brain, making me light-headed and giddy as I wrapped my arms around his neck, kissing him fiercely. He kissed me back with an intensity that should have scared me. Instead, it sent thrills rushing from my head to my toes.

His hands fumbled with the clasp of my bra between my shoulder blades, and the undergarment slid forward. "Let me see them," he demanded, pushing me back so that he could lift my shirt and bra over my head. His eyes glowed in the darkness, and the stark hunger in his irises made me shiver in anticipation. "I love your breasts," he whispered, taking one in each palm, squeezing them gently.

"You do?" I asked before I could stop myself. Normally, I didn't show any kind of weakness in the bedroom, but we were making love in a horse stall, and I'd always thought my breasts were a little on the small side.

"Yes." He licked my right nipple, and I gasped. "They're perfect."

I slid my fingers into Hunter's hair as he lavished my breasts with attention, biting, sucking, and nibbling on my sensitive nipples until I was squirming in his lap. His mouth was hot against my skin, sending molten tendrils of heat into my core until I was throbbing with the need to have him inside me.

"This is no fair," I gasped, pulling away. "You're having all the fun." I scrambled back a few inches from Hunter, and I grinned at his befuddled expression before reaching for his belt. "It's my turn to have some fun."

Hunter relaxed a little, leaning back against the wall. "All right," he said casually, but the gleam of hunger in his eyes betrayed him. "You can give it a go."

His eyes brightened a little as I freed his

cock from his pants. I paused to admire the thick, rigid length of him for a moment.

"Like what you see?" Hunter asked, pumping his hips suggestively.

He waggled his eyebrows at me, and I rolled my eyes, grinning.

"I'd answer, but I have a feeling you don't really need your ego stroked," I teased, wrapping my fingers around his cock. "Let's see if I can stroke something else instead."

I started stroking him, slowly at first, working up to a steady rhythm. I made sure to slide my thumb over his mushroom tip, a particularly sensitive spot. Though Hunter's face tightened a little and he watched me avidly, he gave no other sign that he was feeling anything.

"So, you think you're going to hold out on me, huh, cowboy?" I raised an eyebrow as I stroked him faster. "Well, I'm getting kind of hungry now, and you're looking pretty tasty to me." I leaned down and flicked the tip of my tongue across his head, giving him a seductive smile when he jerked.

"Do your worst," he challenged, a gleam in his eye.

Without breaking eye contact, I settled

onto my elbows between his legs and began licking his shaft. I started by flicking my tongue across the head again and then slowly dragging my tongue from base to tip, covering his cock from all sides. Hunter trembled a little each time I licked him, but he stubbornly clenched his jaw to keep from making any sound.

Well, that's about to change real fast.

I gently bit down on the head. He gasped, and without warning, I took the entire length of him into my mouth, sucking hard. The response was instantaneous. Hunter bucked beneath me, his hands fisting in my hair as he hissed. I showed no mercy, thoroughly sucking him and massaging his balls with my free hand. His sac grew tighter in my hand until I knew he was on the verge of exploding.

"Stop," Hunter gasped. "I'm not ready yet. I need to be inside you."

I considered resisting his wishes, but he reasserted his dominance by yanking me up by the hair and tossing me to the ground. In seconds, my jeans and panties were down by my ankles and then thrown somewhere into the darkness. Then he reached into his wallet, yanking out a condom, tearing it open, and sheathing his huge cock. He eased it inside me, filling me completely.

"Oh God," I gasped, clinging to him.

He pulled out and thrust back in, sending another spark of pleasure through me.

"You're so big."

"Shit!" Hunter stilled and then pulled out a little. "Am I hurting you?"

I shook my head, sinking my hands into his ass so I could push him back inside me again. "No. You feel good. More," I encouraged.

He began thrusting inside me again. The throbbing inside me eased and then increased with every thrust, pushing me closer and closer to the edge of bliss. But I held on, wanting this moment to last as long as it could.

"Your pussy feels so good," he rasped, staring down at me.

I gazed into his gemlike eyes, sucked into the storm of emotion and hunger I saw there that mirrored my own feelings so well. Wanting more, I increased the pace, forcing him to match my thrusts as we raced closer to the end. All too soon, it came, but the blinding rush of pleasure was so all-consuming that I was filled with bliss from head to toe, something that had never happened to me in my entire life.

When I finally came back to myself, Hunter was lying on top of me, pressing me into the dirt and hay as he caught his breath, and I realized he must have come too. Gently, I stroked his back through his shirt, and we lay there for a long while as our heart rates evened out.

"That was incredible," Hunter said finally, levering himself up onto his elbows to look at me. The raw hunger in his face was replaced by a peaceful expression, his facial muscles relaxing.

"Yeah, it was." I stroked the side of his face, enjoying the way his stubble teased the backs of my fingers.

"Especially the hellacious light show," he muttered under his breath.

"What?"

"Nothing, darling," he answered with a smile. "Just a hallucination I had while experiencing the best sex of my entire life."

"Your entire life, huh?" I arched a brow.

"Hell yes!"

"Well, goddamn! I feel special."

"You are special," he answered before kissing me hard on the lips. "To me," he finished before pulling back to stare at me.

My heart raced, and my tummy got tied up in knots from his unexpected compliment.

"You know, Hunter...you've seen me naked twice, and I haven't seen you naked yet."

Hunter laughed and then reared up onto his knees. "Well, I can't promise you a full show right now," he said, his eyes twinkling as he discarded the condom and buttoned up his jeans, "on account of wanting to be prepared and everything, but I guess I can take my shirt off for you."

He slowly unbuttoned his flannel shirt, revealing a tawny expanse of chest and washboard abs that I could definitely do laundry on. He allowed the shirt to slip down his broad shoulders and then stood still as I came closer, enabling me to inspect him by the light of the moon.

"Do I meet your standards?" he asked, his amusement evident.

I ran my fingers through the curls on his

chest and then followed the happy trail disappearing down beneath the waistband of his jeans. His lower abs tightened a little as my fingers hovered there, barely dipping below, and I swore I saw his manhood swell a little beneath the denim.

"I think you'd meet most male-model industry standards, yes," I teased. Then I smoothed my hands back up his chest and down his shoulders, running them along the dips and valleys of his triceps. "Shit, would I love to photograph you sometime," I murmured, entranced by his muscle definition.

"Maybe you can."

"Huh?" I glanced up at him in surprise, but there was no mockery or sarcasm in his expression.

"Maybe you can photograph me sometime," he said, smiling. "I've never posed nude before, but I'd be willing to do it for you," he said, waggling his eyebrows again.

I laughed. "I haven't had to photograph a nude male in a while, but I have a feeling I'd enjoy doing you."

Hunter raised a brow. "I'm pretty sure we've discovered that you already enjoy doing me," he said as he snagged me by the waist, covering my mouth with a bone-melting kiss.

"Smartass," I muttered against his lips before he lowered me to the hay-covered ground again.

18

HUNTER

"Hey, sunshine," I called while walking in through the front door. "Guess what?"

"You're tracking mud all over the floor again?" Mrs. Jones answered for Kia, who was already sitting at the table eating dinner after a long day of work.

The woman didn't even look up from what she was doing and didn't see the face I made at her or that I wiped my shoes on the mat a second time before crossing the space between the front door and the dining room.

"No, actually," I said slowly, pulling out a chair and seating myself, "I was going to tell Kia that I have a surprise for her. But if she's not interested..." I trailed off, reaching for the pork roast on the table.

"A surprise?" Kia's face lit up, and she dropped her fork, her food forgotten.

Her face was freshly scrubbed, and for a moment, I was entranced by the healthy glow emanating from her skin. Her spirits had come way up since the first night we'd made love in the stall, which was nearly a week ago. She'd thrown herself back into the ranch work wholeheartedly and came to sleep with me every night, which delighted me. A part of me knew I should make her sleep in the house—where it was warmer, more comfortable, and in case of a wolf attack, much safer—but I couldn't bring myself to send her away. Plus, I enjoyed her company and our nightly candid chats in the barn, where we shared our most intimate sexual fantasies and created a menu of the type of erotic activities we wanted to try.

"Well, that is what I said." I served myself a scoop of mixed vegetables. "But I can see you're hungry, so maybe we'll just wait."

There was silence for all of thirty seconds before Kia blurted out, "What kind of surprise is it?"

"That would be telling," I said, waggling my eyebrows, a habit I knew pushed Kia's buttons.

"Oh, for Christ's sake," Kia huffed, tossing down her napkin and standing up. "Let's go see what it is, then. This'd better not be some kind of prank."

I grinned and hurried after her so I could open the front door for her. "This way," I said. Taking her by the hand, I started leading her to the stables.

"What? Have you finally decided to install a bed or something?" Kia teased.

Then she fell silent as I led her to Twilight's stall. Inside was a beautiful chestnut quarter horse with large, dark eyes and a splash of white on its nose.

"Say hello to her," I prompted. "She's our newest cutting horse trainee."

"She's beautiful." Kia gently stroked the horse's muzzle, and the animal closed its eyes, seeming to enjoy the attention. "What's her name?"

"I thought maybe you'd like to decide."

Kia pursed her lips, studying the horse in the lantern light I held aloft, and then said, "I think Sunset. Her coat is a nice deep color, and sunset comes before twilight." She smiled, but it quickly disappeared as she turned to me with a frown. "How much—"

I placed a finger to her mouth to silence her. "This isn't charity, Kia," I said, knowing what she was thinking before she even said a word about it. "I'm an investor, remember? And in order to make sure this business is profitable by the end of the month, I decided it would be in the best interest of the ranch if I replaced Twilight."

The left corner of Kia's mouth curled up. "Are you done lecturing me yet?"

I dropped my finger from her mouth, grinning sheepishly. "Sorry. I just didn't want you to bite my head off."

Kia lifted my hand and pressed a kiss to my knuckles. "I'd never bite your head off," she said seriously. "Now, other parts, however..."

She waggled her eyebrows in a perfect imitation of me, and I laughed.

"All right, you little vixen," I said, taking her by the hand and leading her back to the house, "let's go finish dinner before Mrs. Jones comes out here and finds us in some kind of compromising position."

My cell rang, so I quickly pulled it out of my pocket, giving it a glance. It was Matt returning my call.

I kissed her on the nose. "Go on in, darling. I have to take this call."

She slapped me on the ass. "Don't take too long, cowboy," she replied before striding away, leaving me gawking at the sexy jiggle of her ass.

"Damn, woman!" I yelled out to her. "Have I told you that you have an amazing ass?"

She laughed huskily. "Yep. Every time I'm riding you. Hashtag, tap it," she responded loudly before disappearing into the house.

"What the fuck, Matt?" I hissed into my cell while walking far enough away from the house so that my conversation couldn't be overheard. "I left you a voice message hours ago. Thank God I wasn't fucking dying."

"I'm at a poker tournament," he growled. "What's up?"

"Something strange happened to me during sex."

"Oh, for fuck's sake! You called me to brag about your latest kinky conquest? I don't have time for this shit, Hunter. I have to get back to the tournament."

"Matt, will you shut the hell up and just listen? It's not about sex. It's about a hallucination that I had during it. Well, it's that... and the incessant ranting of my inner wolf about her being our true mate." I launched into telling him about the light show I had experienced while making love to Kia. I detailed the strange vision of the swirling kaleidoscopes that formed two separate figures before merging into one, drawing all the colors into a big sphere that eventually burst into shimmering light. "So, am I going batshit crazy? And what the fuck is a true mate?"

"Well, first, you are batshit crazy. I've been telling you that shit for years."

"Fuck off," I grumbled.

"Look," Matt started, "on a more serious note, your wolf might be right about her being your true mate. Because that little light show that you saw? Well, Gunner told me he experienced the same shit with Celine, but he didn't understand what it was. So, he called Eli."

"And?" I prodded impatiently.

"Eli told Gunner that every pure-blooded shifter has a true mate—the one person who completes them. You know, equivalent to that sappy soul-mate shit. But—"

I cut him off. "That makes no sense. Why would I have a vision like that if I'm not a pureblood?"

"Are you going to let me finish or not?" Matt barked.

"Go ahead," I growled.

"As I was about to say, Eli got his info wrong. Celine had to set him and Gunner straight. She told them that all shifters, regardless of whether they are purebloods or hybrids, have a true mate. The problem is that not very many ever find theirs."

"Holy shit!" I exclaimed.

This news wasn't good on many levels. But most importantly because Kia had been terrified and traumatized by what she called a monster. I knew there was no way in hell she would accept the fact that I was a hybrid wolf-shifter, much less want to still be with me.

"Yep, holy shit." Matt started laughing. "Damn! I can't wait to tell the rest of the guys that you found your mate and that you're officially off the fuck-everything-that-moves team. So, is she a hybrid?"

"No. She's human," I muttered.

"Wait...what?"

"You heard me," I replied, "and the most fucked-up part is that, when she was young, a shifter killed her mother."

"Damn, bro!" Matt exclaimed. "So, when are you going to tell her you're a hybrid shifter?"

Never.

Damn...my life is so fucked right now.

19

KIA

"Miss Nash!" Mrs. Jones called from the front porch. "Phone call for you!"

I looked up from the hoof I was currently cleaning out and then stood up so I could peer over the rump of the palomino I was grooming. Sure enough, Mrs. Jones was standing there, waving at me.

"I'll be right there," I called. Then I bent my head to the task. I finished with the hoof I was working on and patted the palomino's shoulder, leaving her tied to the corral post. I'd make this quick and then get back to the chore, so I could get all the horses groomed before Hunter came back from training.

"Do you know who it is?" I asked Mrs. Jones as I jogged up the steps.

"He said his name was Drew Stevens, your personal assistant."

Drew was my right-hand man, and while I was in Texas, he was handling my business and personal financial affairs. We'd also agreed that while I was away, he'd contact me only in an emergency. Anxiety fluttered in the pit of my belly, but I refused to let it show, simply thanking Mrs. Jones and heading to the phone in the living room. I sat down in the recliner and picked up the phone, wondering what Drew could possibly be calling me about and why he didn't ring my cell.

Damn. My cell is probably dead. The last time I used my phone, the battery was low. I couldn't remember if I charged it or not.

"Hello?"

"Kia!" Drew sounded relieved. "I'm so glad I finally got you on the phone. Your cell kept going straight to voice mail. Listen, I tried to make one of your condo loan payments today, and your bank said there weren't enough funds in the account."

"Shit!" I pinched the bridge of my nose,

already feeling the pressure building up in my sinuses. I'd had Drew pay all my bills for me out of my savings account, and I guessed there was less money than I'd thought. "Is the payment past due yet?"

"No, you've still got a day," Drew said. "Do you want me to get on the phone and ask for an extension?"

"No." I'd already been late once or twice before, and I didn't want to get in bad standing with any of my creditors. "Um...use my credit card. There should be enough on there to cover it." I told him where to find it and then hung up the phone and put my head in my hands.

Two more weeks. Only two more weeks, and then I can get back home and start making some money. But do I really want to leave?

I was actually starting to enjoy the simplicity of ranch life. While I did miss my photography, there were no high-maintenance models for me to deal with. No high-stress gigs or tight deadlines while I was out here. There was only wide-open space, farm animals, good Texas food, and Hunter.

Hunter.

I was going to miss him like hell when I

left. I'd never had such a thorough and attentive lover in my life, nor slept as well as I did after a bout of lovemaking with him, which was saying something, considering I was spending most of my nights on a stable floor. When I wasn't working, I was with him, and when I was working, I often found myself daydreaming about him.

Is this what love is?

I walked back out to the corral in a daze. I'd never been in love before, never allowed myself to get close enough to a man for such a thing to happen, and the idea both terrified and thrilled me.

But, mostly, it just made me sad because I knew a relationship between Hunter and me would never work. He was a cowboy, and I was a New York City girl. I knew he was never going to give up his ranches to move to the city with me. And, even if he were willing, I wouldn't want him to. It was clear as day to me that he belonged here, and I wasn't going to keep him from what he loved.

✵ 20 ✵

HUNTER

"Darling," I murmured into Kia's hair. "You have to tell me what's wrong."

Kia responded by burrowing her face more firmly into my chest, turning her cheek toward my armpit so that I couldn't meet her gaze. "I don't have to do anything," she muttered.

I gently slid two fingers beneath Kia's chin, forcing her to meet my gaze. "Kia," I implored, "you've been moody for the last couple of days, you haven't wanted to have sex, and you've hardly spoken two words to me."

"Maybe I'm on my period," Kia said snidely.

She tried to turn away again, but I held fast.

"No, I don't think that's it." While the dark cloud of emotion that had settled over Kia could certainly be explained that way, my sense of smell told me that time of the month hadn't arrived yet. "Something's been bothering you for the last couple of days, and you won't tell me what it is."

Kia simply glared at me, and I met her stare evenly, not willing to back down.

Finally, she sighed and dropped her gaze. "Hunter, do you love me?"

"What?" The question caught me off guard.

She met my gaze again, a challenging look in her eye. "It's a simple damn question."

I didn't say anything for a few moments, not sure how to respond. "I guess I don't know," I answered honestly. "I've never been in love before."

Kia bit her lip. "Neither have I. But I do know I've never been this close to anyone in my life."

She stroked my bare upper arm, and my inner wolf howled in response, making me want to arch my back in pleasure.

"Yeah, same here." I wasn't sure where this conversation was going, and I also wasn't sure I liked it, but I wasn't going to risk hurting Kia's feelings by saying so.

The truth was, I knew I was falling in love with her, but I didn't know if I was ready to admit it, not after the story she'd told me about the shifter who'd killed her mother. There was no way I was going to commit myself to a relationship with her without telling her what I really was, and I didn't know whether or not it was safe enough to do that. Though I'd always considered myself pretty tough, Kia had wormed her way into a place inside me no one had ever been before, and I wasn't sure if I would survive rejection from her.

"I don't think this is a good thing," she whispered.

"What?"

"These feelings we're developing... I don't think they're a good thing," Kia repeated. Determination hardened her eyes, the earlier sadness completely gone. "In two weeks, our bet is up, and no matter which way the chips fall, I'm going back to New York, and you're staying here."

Anger blazed in my heart at the idea that Kia was going to leave me, and my wolf roared in displeasure, but I managed to rein in my emotions. "You could always stay here," I blurted without thinking.

Kia arched an eyebrow. "You'd want me to leave behind my life's work for you, wouldn't you?" she sneered. Then she rolled out of my arms and stood up. She brushed the hay from her clothing and straightened her shoulders. "Well, I've got news for you, Hunter. I've got no plans to give up my photography career...just like you have no plans to give up your life as a rancher."

She set her jaw, daring me to challenge her statement, but I said nothing. She was one hundred percent right, and I wasn't about to do her the discourtesy of lying or making false promises.

When it became clear that I wasn't going to answer her, she relaxed a little. "The sooner we both come to terms with this, the better," she said quietly. Then she turned on her heel and walked out.

I stared up at the wooden slats of the ceiling for a long time, and by the time I fell asleep, I still didn't have an answer for her.

❧ 21 ☙

KIA

I WAS COLLECTING eggs from the chicken coop to sell at the weekly farmers market when I heard the sound of a car pulling up at the front of the house. A rooster tried to peck at my hand, and I swatted him away before collecting the three eggs from the nest in front of me. Gathering up my basket, I headed around the front to investigate.

I wonder who it could be.

Hunter had sold two of the horses and was out delivering them to a rancher who lived several hours away, so there was no way he was back already, and Mrs. Jones had gone to visit her sister and wasn't due back for at least two hours. But my question was answered quickly enough when I spotted the black sedan out front, and my spine stiffened involuntarily as the dark-haired man got out of the car with briefcase in hand.

"Miss Nash!" Samuel Bradley called, flashing me a perfect smile.

He was wearing sunglasses today, so I couldn't see his eyes, but I was sure they were just as icy and crafty-looking as they'd been the last time he was here.

"Mr. Bradley," I responded coolly, planting myself between the car and the porch steps in a way that made it clear I wasn't about to invite him inside. "I can't imagine what possibly could have brought you here today."

"I just wanted to come by and see if I could discuss some of the finer points with you in case you do decide to sell."

"If I do decide to sell, it certainly won't be to you," I informed him coldly.

"And why exactly," he said slowly, "is that?"

"I instinctively dislike you, and I don't do business with people I don't like." That wasn't entirely true. I worked with models and fashion reps all the time that I detested, but that was a different career, and besides, it sounded like a Texan thing to say. I was certain Hunter would be proud.

Stop that. I don't care whether or not Hunter would be proud.

It had been three days since I last slept in the stables, and the two of us had maintained a respectful distance.

That is a good thing.

I was determined to ignore the constant ache in my heart, demanding I take him into my arms and never let him go. If I kept ignoring it, it would eventually go away.

Mr. Bradley flashed me a sharklike grin that sent a shiver up my spine. "Well, that's a pretty silly way to do business, especially considering you'd be missing out on a hell of a deal without even knowing what it was."

"And what deal would that be?" I asked, intrigued in spite of myself.

"Well, I'd really prefer to go inside and discuss it." When I hesitated, he scoffed. "Please, I'm not going to bite. And it's not as if you don't have any means to defend yourself," he said, eyeing the gun holstered at my hip.

I'd taken to carrying it ever since the last

time he visited, not wanting to be caught defenseless again while I was alone on the ranch.

"Fine." I stepped aside, giving him access to the porch steps. "You first." No way was I giving this man my back.

He flashed me another smile and then moved past me, heading up the steps and letting himself into the house. I led him to the dining table and thought about offering him tea or coffee but then decided against it, not wanting to leave him alone for a moment.

Not that he looks like the type who needs to steal. I eyed his expensive suit and platinum cuff links. *But one can never be too careful.*

"So," I said, clasping my hands together above the table, "tell me what it is you're so desperate to offer."

He arched a brow, acknowledging my jab. He'd taken off his glasses, and he observed me with his shrewd gaze for a moment before he spoke, "It occurred to me that you might be curious about my intentions toward the ranch."

"That would be one way of putting it." Suspicious was more like it, but I held my tongue, wanting to hear what he had to say.

"I know that your company likes to buy up failing ranches and other properties and then turn them into housing developments."

He nodded. "It's true that we make the bulk of our profits that way," he acknowledged, "but the truth is that I'm not here on behalf of Bradley and Radcliffe. I'm actually interested in this property on a personal level."

"Is that so?" I found that hard to believe. "What would a man like you want with a working ranch?"

"Well, normally, I would never consider buying a property like this for my own personal use," Samuel said, lowering his voice conspiratorially. "But the reason I'm so interested in this specific property is because a good source told me this place is sitting on a gold mine."

"A gold mine?" I sat up straighter. "What kind of gold mine?" I couldn't imagine there were actual gold deposits beneath the ground, though I supposed anything was possible.

"Oil."

I barely managed to keep my jaw from dropping. *The ranch is sitting on top of an oil well?* Dollar signs began prancing through my head at the idea of the potential wealth. I could pay back all my debts and then some. I could open studios across the city. I could—

"Wait a minute," I said, coming back to my senses. "You want to buy the ranch and turn it into an oil field?"

"That's the idea," Samuel said. "I'm not planning on becoming a rancher after all."

My heart dropped into my stomach. The ranch would be completely destroyed, which was exactly what my great-uncle hadn't wanted. But I didn't say that to Samuel, knowing he would just argue the point.

"If that's true," I said slowly, "then why on earth would I want to sell the ranch to you? I could just drill the oil myself and keep all the profits."

"That's true," he said, "but oil drilling is an expensive venture, and I doubt you have the capital to get it going. I, on the other hand, have connections to the oil-drilling industry, as well as the financial resources to get such a project going, and I am in an infinitely better position than you to capitalize on the potential wealth of this ranch."

I opened my mouth to tell him that I had

a resource in the oil industry as well and then stopped. I didn't actually know Hunter's brother, Eric, on a personal level, and there was no way he was going to step in and help me with a project that would go directly against Hunter's wishes.

A project you aren't even interested in doing anyway, my conscience reminded me.

Guilt flooded my chest.

"I must admit, I was pretty surprised at your initial offer of one hundred thousand dollars," I said. "But now that you've explained the situation to me, it sounds like a pretty pitiful sum."

"I agree," he said. "That is why I'm now prepared to offer you five hundred thousand dollars, as well as ten percent of all future profits."

I felt as if my head was going to explode. *Five hundred thousand dollars...plus ten percent of the millions of dollars that Mr. Bradley was going to make in the future?*

How on earth can I turn down all that money?

"You must be dead certain there's oil on this land," I countered.

"I have a very good source," he insisted while opening up the briefcase he'd set on the table. He pulled out a several-page legal document. "Here's a contract with all the particulars. It's not an official bill of sale, but it does outline the exact agreement."

I knew I shouldn't take the contract, but my fingers curled around it anyway. "I can't sign anything right now," I said, infusing my voice with conviction I was no longer certain I felt.

"Of course," he said smoothly. "I just wanted to update my offer and give you this document so you would have a chance to look it over yourself—and with a lawyer, if you would like." He stood up, and I hastily followed suit. "I'm sorry to be abrupt, but I have to get going now."

"I'll show you out." I walked him to the door, the contract still clutched in my hand, and followed him out to the porch so I could watch him get in his car. My instincts, which hadn't quite been overruled by greed, still told me he couldn't be trusted, and I didn't want to let him out of my sight.

He paused on the top step and looked back at me, his glasses once more shielding his gaze from me. Nevertheless, a chill still raced through me.

"You know, any current agreement you've made with Hunter Golden is not legally binding. So, you can still let him in on this business opportunity." He grinned, trotted down the steps, got into his car, and drove off.

I stared off into space for a long moment and then jumped as one of the roosters crowed, startling me out of my damn wits. Remembering my chore, I raced to the back-yard to finish collecting the eggs and put the contract out of my mind.

HUNTER

I SLAMMED the truck door shut behind me and then checked the paper bag in my hand, making sure everything I'd picked up from the grocery store was still safely tucked in there. Satisfied that my toolbox was fully stocked, I stalked up the stairs and into the house, determined to find Kia and break down the walls between us.

It had been barely a week since she'd walked out on me in the stalls and erected a barrier between us, but to me, it felt like a lifetime. And every time I tried to take baby steps to repair our relationship, it had only caused her to withdraw from me further. Now, with only a few days left until our bet was finished, I knew I was on the cusp of losing her, and I couldn't let that shit happen.

Drastic measures were going to be taken tonight, and as far as I was concerned, nothing was out of bounds if it meant getting Kia back.

As expected, Kia was pacing back and forth in the kitchen, worrying her lip with her teeth. As soon as she caught sight of me, she whirled around, stalking toward me.

"Where on earth is Mrs. Jones?" she asked, her voice shrill with worry. "I came back in an hour ago to find that she was gone, and she's not in the back cottage outside. I can't find her anywhere!"

"That's because I gave her the rest of the day off," I said easily.

"You what?" Kia froze. "Why on earth would you do that?"

"Because tonight is just about you and me." Ducking down, I caught her by the waist, hefting her over my shoulder. Then I turned and headed for the stairs.

"What the hell? Put me down!" Kia began to pound her fists against my back. "I don't want to go upstairs with you. I want to go downstairs and eat dinner!"

"Too bad." I opened the door to her bedroom and somehow managed to close and lock it behind me despite Kia's thrashing. "Mrs. Jones isn't coming back until tomorrow, and you're a horrible cook." I tossed her unceremoniously onto the bed and then put the grocery bag on the nightstand. "Guess you're just going to have to eat what I bought."

"You bought dinner?" Kia eyed the bag skeptically. "Why? And why are we eating up here?"

"It's a special kind of dinner," I said suggestively, sitting next to her on the bed. "And one I think you're going to enjoy."

Perching on the edge of the bed, I started unpacking the grocery bag and bit back a grin when Kia's eyes widened.

"Is that whipped cream?" she asked, sounding scandalized, but I didn't miss the undercurrent of excitement in her tone. "And strawberries?"

"It sure is." I plucked a strawberry from the container, dabbed it in the whipped cream, and held it up. "You want some?"

Kia reached for it, but I placed the leaves in my mouth and bit down so that the strawberry was hanging from my lips. "Come and get it," I said around the mouthful.

Kia stared at the berry for a long moment, and I waited in anticipation to see what she would do. For a moment, I thought she would lunge for the box on the nightstand, but ever-so-slowly, she leaned over and took a small bite out of the berry. Her eyes fluttered closed for a moment as pleasure flushed her cheeks, and I bit back a groan when she licked the whipped cream off her lips. She leaned in for another bite and then another until the berry was finally finished, and there was no mistaking the pulse fluttering at her throat in reaction to the sweet fruit. Being this close to her without touching her was testing every inch of my willpower, and I had no doubt it was doing the same to her.

"I...we shouldn't be doing this," she whispered, but she didn't resist when I gently pushed her back on the bed.

"This was one of the erotic fantasies you told me about during our nights in the barn, right?" I asked as I grabbed another strawberry. This time, I dipped it in chocolate sauce and held it just above her mouth, allowing the chocolate to drip onto her luscious lips. "The one where a guy covers you in chocolate and whipped cream and strawberries and then licks it all off your body?"

"I didn't think you remembered," she gasped as I slid the chocolate-coated berry down her throat. Then I licked the area clean with my tongue. I repeated the process, dabbing the sensitive spots of her collarbone with the strawberry and then lapping up the chocolate residue.

"I've been thinking about it ever since, and I was trying to figure out a way to make it happen in the stables before you left," I confessed, feeding her the strawberry.

A trickle of strawberry juice gushed from her lips and down her chin, and I licked it off unhurriedly, enjoying the way she trembled beneath my tongue.

"Then I decided, if you were going to be leaving me in a few days, there was no way I was going to let you go...not without fulfilling your fantasy."

"Hunter," she moaned as I dabbed her earlobe with a bit of whipped cream.

I sucked on it. She writhed beneath me, and I delighted in the rush of power I felt at holding her captive this way, mentally and physically. I'd played with food and sex before, of course, covering my cock in honey and making my current piece of ass lick it off, but there was something so much better about being the giver than the recipient. At least, there was with Kia.

When I got her all nice and riled up, I pulled away from her long enough to strip off her clothing. Then I returned with the can of whipped cream. With a devilish smile, I coated her nipples liberally and then sprayed a path down the center of her cleavage and stopped at her belly button where I left a particularly generous dollop. The scent of Kia's arousal was thick in the air as she watched me, her body trembling in anticipation. When I finally lowered my mouth to lick the whipped cream off her left nipple, she moaned, and the sound was music to my ears.

"Ooh," she moaned, clutching my head to her breast.

I lavished attention on each nipple, moving over, lapping, and sucking at the cream on her belly. I dipped my tongue into her belly button, chuckling at her squeal when I swirled my tongue around to get all the cream there. But when I spread her legs, she sat up with a gasp.

"You're not going to...oh!" she squealed as I sprayed a generous amount onto her clit, careful to avoid her lips.

I immediately started licking and sucking at the area, showing absolutely no mercy as she screamed, her hips bucking against my face. I slid two fingers inside her, stroking her inner walls just the way she liked, until she came apart in my arms, crying out my name.

"You are mine," I told her, stripping off my clothes and then sheathing my cock with a condom and mounting her.

She eagerly embraced me, not a shred of resistance within her, and I groaned out loud as her throbbing pussy clenched around my cock, nearly undoing me.

"All mine."

I fucked her hard and fast, letting out all my frustration, anger, and desperation at once, and she took it all, meeting me thrust for thrust, clawing at my back, whispering dirty talk in my ear, and urging me on. Wanting to go even deeper, I pulled out and flipped her onto her stomach. Then I grabbed her hair and pulled her head back as I slid into her from behind. She seemed to like this too, grinding her ass into my pelvis as I fucked her, and part of me wondered how I had ever been satisfied with any of the women I'd fucked in the past. I'd done all kinds of things with them, much raunchier than anything I'd tried with Kia so far, yet something as simple as pulling on her hair and fucking her doggy style was enough to undo me.

"I want to hear you come, baby," I growled in her ear, reaching around and massaging her clit.

I pleasured her with my hand and my cock, soaking up each cry and moan, and when she came, her pussy clenching hard around my cock, I followed suit, coming hard in a blinding rush of pleasure that stole my breath and what was left of my mental faculties.

I came back to myself a minute later and frowned when I noticed Kia was trying to inch out from underneath me.

"Where are you going?" I asked, rolling onto my side and hauling her against me.

She stilled in my arms, and I ground my teeth at the tension I could feel thrumming through her body.

"I figured we were done," she said carefully. "Now that you've fulfilled my fantasy and all."

"We are *not* done," I growled, turning her around so that I could look into her eyes. In them, I saw fear and insecurity, and my heart ached fiercely with the need to take away her pain. "I didn't come here just so that we could have one last night before we have to go our separate ways, Kia. I came here because I realized I can't bear to see you go, and I need to make you understand how much you mean to me. I fucking love you, baby."

Kia's lips parted, and tears glimmered in her eyes before she blinked them away. "You can't mean that," she murmured. "You just can't."

"Why can't I?" I asked gently, stroking the curve of her back.

"Because it's going to break my heart when I have to leave you."

"Just because you have to go back to New York doesn't mean you have to leave me." I kissed her nose. "You might not realize this, but I'm kind of a wealthy guy, and I have a lot of resources. There's no reason I can't divide my time between here and New York so I can be with you."

"But your ranches," Kia protested, confusion in her eyes. "Don't you have, like, twenty of them to manage?"

"Yes." I nipped at her chin. "And I can always hire on another manager to help me. I know a few guys." I winked.

"You really mean it, don't you?" she asked in wide-eyed astonishment. "You would cut back on your time out here to come and live with me?"

"Hell yes, I would!" I grinned. "Besides, at least a third of my time was spent traveling and blowing my money on booze and beautiful women," I told her. "Now that I've settled my sights on you, I'll have a lot more time freed up."

"Is that a marriage proposal?" Kia asked, arching an eyebrow.

"Not yet," I said softly. Then I pressed a kiss to her lips. "I don't think you're ready for that yet, especially since you haven't even decided whether or not you love me," I teased.

Kia rolled her eyes. "Of course I—"

The shrill scream of a horse cut her off, and it was like déjà vu all over again with both of us jumping off the bed, rushing toward the window. But this time, I didn't bother to peer out of the glass or rush down the stairs. Instead, I quickly shifted into my beast and then jumped straight through the window. I was consumed by the desire to get to the shifter before he killed another horse.

I landed on the ground in a crouch, amidst a spray of glass, and then sprinted toward the stables, much faster in my hybrid form than as a human. My night vision easily spotted the open stall door, and I launched myself at the shifter who was attacking the palomino, barely avoiding getting his skull crushed by the frantic horse.

"You fucking bastard!" I growled, using inhuman strength to lift the shifter and toss him straight out of the building.

The shifter landed on its feet, a hulking wolf with glowing yellow eyes and fangs. We both charged each other at the same time, clashing in a ball of fur, fangs, and claws as we rolled around, fighting for the upper hand. The wolf's claws scrabbled against my shirt as he snapped at me, but I sank my own clawed hand into the wolf's throat and tightened my grip, squeezing.

"Oh my God!" Kia screamed.

I cursed inwardly at the realization that she was just a few feet away, watching the fearsome battle. I didn't dare look away from the wolf, though. One misstep and the shifter would rip my throat out. Instead, I leaned forward, sinking my fangs into the wolf's shoulder, causing it to howl in pain. The shifter thrashed furiously against me, but I refused to loosen the grip on either his jaw or his hand, and eventually, the shifter passed out, morphing from a gargantuan wolf into a gaunt human with black hair and pale skin.

A loud thud behind me told me that Kia, too, had passed out, and I sighed, resigning myself to a very long and unpleasant night.

❧ 23 ❧

KIA

I woke up on the couch to see Hunter's face hovering over me. It took my mind a few minutes to catch up with what I'd seen before I passed out, and when it did, horror engulfed me, driving all rational thought out of my mind.

"Get the fuck away from me!" I shrieked, backing up to the other end of the couch. I held my hands out, as if I could ward Hunter off. "You're a monster!"

Hurt flashed across Hunter's features, but he didn't refute my claim. "I'm sorry you had to see that," he said quietly, "and we can discuss it later, but for now, there's something else we need to focus on."

"No, there isn't." I was hyperventilating now, and I fanned my face, trying to take in deep breaths. All I could see was Hunter's face as he'd transformed into that half-man, half-beast thing and jumped out the window...just like my mother's killer. "The only thing you need to do is get the hell out of this house and never come back."

"Oh, yeah?" Hunter challenged, taking a step forward. "And just what do you want to do about that guy?" He jabbed a finger out to his left.

I slowly followed his gaze and then let out a gasp at the sight of a man trussed up in one of the kitchen chairs with a length of rope. He was naked but for a pair of boxers that I recognized as some of Hunter's, and his expression was resigned as his dark eyes glanced between Hunter and me.

"I'm guessing you never told her about what you were?" the stranger said dryly.

"Oh my fucking God." The puzzle pieces finally clicked into place, and I thought I was going to be sick. "You're the wolf who attacked the horse...who killed Twilight." My head spun for a moment, and I dug my nails into my palms, willing myself to toughen up and stay in the moment. "Is he like the one who attacked my mother?" I asked Hunter.

Hunter shook his head. "Our friend over there is a pure-blooded shifter," he explained. "A human who can shift into the form of a specific animal...or in some rare cases, an animal who can shift into the form of a human." He sneered at the man, who curled his lip at Hunter in return. "The one who attacked your mother and killed her was likely a hybrid shifter. A human who can change into a man-beast shape. From your description, he was probably a hybrid wolf-shifter."

"And what are you?" I asked faintly, not sure if I really wanted to hear the answer. The monster Hunter had turned into seemed like a combination of man-beast, so that had to mean...

"Yeah, I'm a hybrid wolf-shifter as well, but I'm in control of my animal," Hunter replied carefully, confirming my fear. "I'm half wolf, half human, and, no, I wasn't born that way," he said with an exasperated look. I opened my mouth to ask another question, but he cut me off, "Look, you can grill me all you want later, but right now, there are more important things to worry about." He glared at the man in the chair. "Tell her what you told me."

"My name is Jason Stanley," the man said in a dull tone, as though he were reciting a particularly boring essay or poem. "I'm a pure-blooded wolf-shifter, and I was hired by Samuel Bradley to terrorize and kill off some of your horses so you would sell."

I sat up straight, the fog in my mind suddenly evaporating. "What?" I whispered, unable to believe I'd heard right.

"Samuel Bradley hired me to kill your horses so you'd be forced to sell the ranch," Jason repeated.

"That fucker," I muttered. I dropped my head into my hands. "I can't believe this shit is happening."

"Well, you can believe it, darling," Hunter said, his voice hard.

I raised my head to see that he was staring at me intently.

"I want to make sure you understand that the man who offered you a hundred thousand dollars in order to turn your uncle's ranch into a housing development hired a dangerous shifter to attack in order to force you to do his bidding."

"Yeah...I understand," I said slowly. I rose from the couch and began moving toward the staircase in a dreamlike state. "I understand perfectly."

Hunter caught me by the arm and spun me around. "Where do you think you're going? Don't you have anything to say about this? Don't you think we should decide what to do with him?"

"No," I said. To my ears, my voice sounded like it was coming from a thousand miles away. "You can decide what to do about him. I just need to get away."

Turning around, I headed up the stairs and wished with all my might that, when I came back down the stairs, everything would be normal again, back to the way it had been before I found out that my lover was a damn monster.

24

HUNTER

It was nearly two in the morning by the time I trudged up the stairs to check on Kia. Dread weighed me down, making each step seem like an eternity. Part of me didn't want to see her at all, to have to face the look of horror and loathing in her eyes. But the other part of me ached to make her understand that, while I was a monster, I would never hurt her. I wanted her to look past my beast inside me to the man she'd known all along.

"Kia?" I knocked softly on her bedroom door. Light seeped into the hallway through the crack in the door, so I knew she was awake, but I didn't want to barge in on her, not in the state she was in.

"Come in," she said dully.

The dread increased to the point that it took everything in me to turn the knob and open the door. The sight of Kia sitting up against the headboard, her knees drawn into her chest, as she stared off into space didn't do anything to ease my anxiety.

"What did you do with Jason?" she asked, not looking at me.

"I let him go." The bed creaked under my weight as I perched myself on the edge. I tried to meet Kia's eyes, but she refused to look at me, intent on staring at the wall. "He was a desperate rogue who was starving with no money, and he didn't bear any real ill will toward us. I gave him a bit of money and pointed him in the direction of a wolf-shifter pack." My heart lightened a little at the reminder that I had in fact done a good deed today.

Kia did meet my gaze now, but her eyes were blank, devoid of their usual spark of emotion, and that worried me.

"I see," she said.

I waited for her to say more and then let

out a sigh when she didn't. "Is that all you have to say?" I demanded. "You're not going to address the humongous elephant in the room?"

"You mean, that you're a...wolf-shifter?" Something flickered in her eyes then, but it was gone so fast I wondered if I'd imagined it. "I don't know what else there is to say about it, Hunter. You are what you are."

"Okay..." I said slowly. Then I sighed when Kia returned to staring at the wall. "Look, Kia, if you don't want to be with me anymore, I understand. The bet is over in two days, and since the ranch has turned a profit, we can set up Johnny to take over, and you can be out of here. But we have to address the fact that Samuel Bradley tried to sabotage the ranch, and he needs to be brought to justice for that."

Kia turned to look at me, and this time, there was emotion in her eyes—a slow, simmering rage that caught me off guard. "And just how do you propose we do that?" she asked in a quiet, deadly voice that told me she was about to rip into me.

"My brother, Eric, has been looking into him," I started to say. "With his resources—"

"Samuel has resources too!" Kia shrieked, slapping her hand against the bedspread, her eyes wild now. "You can say whatever you want, but there's no getting around the fact that we can't prove he hired a...*wolf-shifter* to come after us. The authorities would laugh in our faces, just as they laughed in mine when I told them about my mother." She laughed bitterly. "If only they knew what I know now."

My heart ached at the pain in Kia's voice. "Darling..." I began, reaching for her hand.

"Don't touch me," she snapped, snatching her hand away. "You knew all along about the wolf-shifter, didn't you? And you never once told me. That's why you were guarding the stables every night. Because you knew he would come back."

"I suspected," I admitted, shame flooding me. "I didn't want to tell you because I was afraid you would react like this."

"And so I have," Kia said. She was quiet for a long moment. "I don't want anything to do with this mess," she told me. "I tried my best to put this crazy stuff behind me when my mother died, and I won't let it ruin my life."

"It doesn't have to—" I started to say, but she cut me off.

"There's no guarantee that Samuel won't send someone or something just as deadly after me to get what he wants," Kia snapped. "As long as his sights are set on the ranch, neither I nor anyone who works here will be safe. I don't see any reason I should hold out on selling the ranch to him besides simply honoring the memory of someone who isn't around to appreciate it, especially not after the offer he made me."

"You mean, the hundred thousand dollars?" I scoffed. "Kia, if you're that concerned, then I'll buy the ranch from you right now for that amount. Take it off your hands, so you can move on and never look back."

"He offered me five hundred thousand," Kia said flatly. "And ten percent of all future profits."

"He did not." I waited for Kia to tell me it was a joke, but as the seconds ticked by in silence, I realized she was dead serious. "He came to see you again, didn't he?"

Guilt flickered in Kia's eyes for a moment before they turned to ice again. "Last week," she admitted, "while you were out delivering those horses. He claims there's an oil reservoir beneath the land."

"And you're going to sell it to him?" I asked, a tidal wave of rage building inside me at the thought of Daniel's beautiful ranch being turned into an oil field. "Even after he's proven himself to be a degenerate piece of shit?"

"Yes."

"You've got to be kidding, Kia!" The wave of rage burst over me, and I seized Kia by the arms and shook her. "After everything we've worked so hard for, after everything I've done for you, and you're just going to throw it all away? For money!"

"Let go of me!" Kia cried.

But I was past hearing her. My fangs slid out, and even my wolf wanted to sink them into her jugular and rip out her pretty little neck. Only the horror in her wide eyes held me in check.

"You didn't do this for me. You did it for Daniel. Are you really going to kill me for going against your wishes for something I wanted no part of?"

I suddenly let go and backed away from Kia, flattening myself against the wall next to the broken window. "No," I said slowly, my fangs and claws receding. I wasn't going to kill Daniel's last relative, not even for something like this. I knew I could never hurt Kia. "No, you're right. I guess I was a fool to think there was any kind of decency in you. If I learned anything during my time in the Army, it's that no amount of force can make someone truly believe in doing the right thing if they don't want to." I shook my head in disgust. "And you say I'm the monster."

Hurt sparked in Kia's eyes, but I didn't feel a damn thing. I moved past her without a word. Then I paused in the open doorway before looking back at her. "I hope the money is worth it, Miss Nash."

I closed the door, leaving my heart behind me in that room, and headed for home.

❧ 25 ❧

KIA

"HONEY, you really need to do a bit more than just pick at that bowl of porridge," Mrs. Jones chided. "You're starting to resemble a bag of skin and bones, and that's not good for my reputation."

"I know," I sighed, forcing a smile for the housekeeper.

Hunter had paid her salary through the end of the month, so Mrs. Jones would stay until I was gone.

"I just haven't had much of an appetite."

I hadn't had much of a will to do anything since Hunter walked out the door three days ago. At first, I'd been relieved he was gone now that I knew he'd been hiding his true nature from me this whole time, putting me in danger with his monstrous secrets. But as time had passed, I found myself missing his quick smile, the sound of his laughter, the way he teased me at times, and his gentle but firm way with the animals. Often, I found myself turning around with a question on my lips for Hunter, only to remember he wasn't here to give me guidance anymore. Twice, I'd nearly broken down and gone to Golden Cattle Ranch to beg him to come back.

But I knew there was no use in doing that. I'd already called up Samuel Bradley and agreed to sign the papers. He was coming by to deliver them tomorrow. And even if I could find it in me to put my pride aside and grovel before Hunter, it didn't change the fact that I, or anyone else who owned the ranch, would be in danger from Samuel unless I just bit the bullet and sold the damn thing. I despised myself for giving in to the enemy, but I just didn't think it was worth the risk to stand up to him.

Mrs. Jones clucked in disapproval at the measly three bites I'd managed before I pushed back my chair, but I didn't say anything further about it. She and I had already had words about the situation, and while Mrs. Jones didn't completely agree with my viewpoint, she understood. In the end, she had to respect my decision on the matter.

I put on my work boots and went out to do the normal chores of the day—letting out the horses, grooming them, putting feed in their buckets, collecting eggs from the coop, weeding the vegetable garden. Finished with that, I came back into the house, going upstairs to do one of the last renovation projects on my checklist—organizing the hall closet and throwing out any junk.

Mrs. Jones offered to help me, but I waved her off. I wanted solitude, and there was something about the work that was oddly peaceful. I sorted through boxes and bags of clothes and memorabilia, making separate piles for anything that seemed useful, anything I would be able to sell, and anything that was trash. It took me several hours to go through Daniel's things, and I tried hard not to think about the fact that, if Hunter were with me, he would likely have all kinds of stories to tell me about the items.

Nearly done, I pulled out a heavy box that was filled with books and started going through them. Most of them were mystery novels, but a few were leather-bound journals filled with recordings of Daniel's daily life. Curious, I opened one up, and it immediately flipped to an entry that made my heart stop.

8/22

AN UPSTART BY THE NAME OF SAMUEL Bradley came to call upon me today. Slick as a grease spot with a hoity-toity attitude and fancy words. Wanted me to sell the ranch to him, something about an oil field, and offered to cut me in on the profits. I told him I didn't give a hoot about any oil field, that the ranch was mine, and I wasn't digging it up for anything. The bastard was pretty persistent, refusing to leave, until I showed him the business end of my shotgun. That'll teach him to mess with a Texan.

"HOLY SHIT," I BREATHED.

So, Samuel had approached my great-uncle about the ranch. Guilt swamped me as I realized that Hunter was right, and I felt awful about dismissing his suspicions. Frantic to learn more, I flipped through the diary, skimming for any other clues. What I learned next about my uncle floored me. Suddenly, all of the pieces fell into place.

Oh my God. I am such a damn fool.

Leaping to my feet, I raced down the stairs, snatching my car keys from the hook by the door. "I'm going out, Mrs. Jones!"

"Where on earth to?" Mrs. Jones asked, looking up from the table she was dusting.

"To Golden Cattle Ranch!" I slammed the door shut, storming over to my vehicle and jumping in. I drove away like hell on wheels, hoping Hunter was still at the ranch and hadn't yet left for greener pastures.

26

HUNTER

"So, you really don't want to use any of this information I worked so hard to get?" Eric demanded, tapping his finger against the sheaf of papers on my desk.

I shook my head, taking a drag from the cigar in my hand as I leaned back in my office chair. "No," I said slowly. "I'm sorry, but I just can't see the point."

The stack of papers on my desk was a lengthy report from a private investigator Eric had hired to look into Bradley and Radcliffe and contained a mountain of white-collar crimes that I could use to lock the bastard away forever.

"What the hell is that supposed to

mean?" Eric threw up his hands. "So what if that woman of yours is selling the ranch? You can still nail him anyway. The government will seize the ranch, and you can buy it back for dirt cheap. That way, Daniel's legacy won't be destroyed."

I shook my head. "Daniel's legacy has always been meant for Kia, and I won't take that away from her. Bradley promised her ten percent of the profits, and she can live comfortably off that and pursue her dreams."

I wasn't going to pretend that I wasn't still angry with Kia, but it didn't change the fact that I still loved her and didn't want to jeopardize the deal she'd made by having Samuel thrown in jail. For her and her alone, I'd make that sacrifice...but I'd be damned if I was ever going to tell her about it. I didn't need her to know what a fucking bleeding heart I'd become.

"You're a better man than I am," Eric said, shaking his head. He ran a hand through his blond hair, which was cut shorter and more fashionably than mine.

While there was no doubt in anyone's mind that the two of us were brothers, Eric's features were more refined, his face classically handsome, while I possessed a more rugged charm.

"I would have hung them both out to dry, especially after the way she treated you." Eric knew all about my curse.

Though we were two very different people, we still loved each other and trusted each other with most everything, and Eric had proven no different when it came to this aspect of my life.

A knock at the door interrupted us, and Leta stuck her head in.

"Miss Nash is here to see you," she informed me. "She says it's important."

My heart leaped at the thought that Kia was at my doorstep, and part of me wanted to spring out of my chair and rush to the door. But the other half, the part that was still aching over her betrayal, forced me back down into my chair and encased a layer of ice over my heart.

"Tell her I'm not available," I told Leta.

My housekeeper hesitated, surprising me. Leta had been entirely sympathetic when I'd related to her what had happened, leaving out the supernatural elements.

"She said you would say that and told me

to tell you that it's about Daniel." She paused. "She said she knows why he was being blackmailed."

"What?" This time, I did rise out of my chair, shock propelling me to my feet. It crossed my mind that this could be some kind of ploy, but if Kia was sincere, this was important information. Unsure of what to do, I glanced down at Eric.

Eric shrugged. "Can't hurt to see what she has to say."

I nodded, sitting back down again. "Send her in."

I braced myself for my first sight of Kia, but nothing could have prepared me for the sight of the gaunt figure who rushed into my office. The glow of excitement in her face didn't quite mask the shadows beneath her eyes or the fact that her clothes were far looser on her than they had any right to be after only three days, and I had to bite my tongue to keep from asking about her welfare.

"Oh, I'm so glad you haven't left yet! I've got something important to show you." Kia slammed a leather-bound book on the table, wedging herself between the empty visitor's chair on her left and Eric on her right.

My brother cleared his throat, and Kia swung around, startled at the noise.

"Oh, I'm sorry. I didn't see you," she said distractedly.

I was finding it increasingly hard to hold on to my anger. I'd never seen Kia so scatter-brained before, and somehow, her out-of-character behavior was completely adorable.

"You must be Eric."

"I am." Eric lifted an eyebrow, clearly not beguiled the way I was.

I managed to get ahold of myself. "What's this information that you feel is so important to share that you barged onto my ranch, uninvited?"

Kia bit her lip, some of the light going out of her. She placed her hands reverently on the black journal, focusing on it rather than on me. "I found this in Uncle Daniel's closet this afternoon when I was going through his stuff," she said. "It's one of several journals he kept." She opened the journal and then carefully flipped through the pages until she found the particular entry she was looking for. "You should read this," she said, sliding it across the desk to me.

Frowning, I bent over the desk to read the entry, and Eric came around the desk to read over my shoulder.

9/14

MY HEART IS HEAVIER THAN IT HAS BEEN IN A long, long time. I met with Samuel Bradley, and he does indeed have the photographic evidence of Randy and me that he claimed. He demanded a sum of $2,500 every month in exchange for his silence. I have no choice but to pay it or be driven out of town.

I GLANCED UP AT KIA, IN MY HEART already knowing what Daniel was saying but wanting confirmation. "What the hell is this supposed to mean?"

"Uncle Daniel was gay," Kia said softly. "His journals confirm that he had a relationship with a man named Randall Wilson, which ended about half a year before the date of this entry when Randy died of cancer."

"Son of a bitch," I hissed, outraged on behalf of my old friend.

Being gay in Texas was practically a crime, especially in a town like Bramblebush, and if Bradley had spread those photos around, Daniel would have been run out of town or shot to death.

"That miserable fuck. I'm going to kill him!"

"Now, hang on," Eric said, resting a placating hand on my shoulder. "There's no need for that, not with all the dirt we have on him. Let's allow the government to clean up."

"Oh, so you were able to find some evidence of illicit activities!" Kia said delightedly. "Now, you can put him away."

"Wait, you mean you actually want him to go to jail now?" I asked incredulously.

"Fuck yes," Kia scowled. "I had several friends in college who were gay, and now my assistant, Drew, and I know how unfairly they were treated. There's no way I'm doing business with a man who tried to blackmail my uncle by using his sexual orientation against him. I can't do that."

"Eric," I murmured to my brother, "can you go out for a moment? I want to speak to Kia privately."

"Sure." My brother nodded to Kia and then exited the room, closing the door behind him.

The two of us stared at each other for a long while before Kia finally broke the silence. "What do you want to say to me?"

I took a breath. "I just...I want to thank you," I said. "I wanted so badly to have justice for Daniel and to figure out what the hell happened to him, and you've given me that. Despite whatever bad blood there might be between us and whatever you decide to do, I want you to know that I'm eternally grateful for what you've done."

"Oh, Hunter." Kia shook her head ruefully. "I'm the one who should be saying those things, not you. You've done so much for me, and I realized I'd acted no better than a bigot with the way I treated you the night I kicked you off the ranch. The truth is, it doesn't matter what species you are. You're an amazing person, and I love you more than I've ever loved anyone or anything in my life."

I could hardly believe my ears. "You what?"

"I love you, Hunter Golden," Kia said, closing the distance between us and wrapping her arms around my neck. She looked up at me with a radiant smile that made me forget about every single thing, except her. "And I've never said those words to anyone in my life, so you'd best believe them, cowboy."

I crushed my mouth against hers, kissing her fiercely, savoring the feel of her in my arms and the heavenly scent of her that surrounded me. She opened her mouth to mine, and I lost myself in the taste of her, drinking in her essence like a man starved. And when the scent of her arousal teased my nostrils, I backed her up against the office door, pressing my erection against her hip.

"Are we—" Kia started to ask.

Then she gasped as I bit down on her neck, hitting one of her sensitive spots. I reached around her to lock the door and then crouched down on my knees to strip off her jeans and panties.

"Hush," I ordered, lifting one of her legs

and hooking it around my shoulders. "I need to make love to you now."

It had only been a few days since I was last inside her, but it felt like an eternity, and we'd parted on such bad terms after our last lovemaking session that I felt the need to eradicate the memory with something spectacular.

"But your brother...ohh..." she moaned when I dragged my tongue across her folds.

"Is downstairs, likely enjoying his fifth cup of coffee and some of Leta's chocolate chip cookies," I informed her. Then I licked her again. "We can join him afterward if you'd like."

I found her clit and started gently sucking on the sensitive nub, and Kia clapped a hand over her mouth to muffle her cries of pleasure. Sliding two fingers inside her, I teased her to the breaking point, loving the way she tasted, the way she trembled against my mouth as though she were coming apart. When she came a few minutes later, crying my name against her palm, I stood up and swiftly pulled a condom out of my wallet. I undid my pants, tore open the condom wrapper, and sheathed my cock. I thrust inside her before her tremors eased.

"Yes!" Kia cried, throwing her head back against the door as another orgasm ripped through her.

My breath caught in my throat at the sight of her parted lips and flushed cheeks, and I bent down to capture her cries of pleasure in my mouth as I fucked her against the oak door. She slid her hands down the back of my jeans, digging her fingers into my ass as she urged me on, and then I was coming, white-hot jets of pleasure shooting through me as I groaned into her mouth.

"I would say that the next time we do this, we're in our honeymoon bed," I panted raggedly a few minutes later, my forehead pressed into the crook of her shoulder as we fought for breath. "But I don't think I can wait that long."

"Wait...what?" Kia lifted my face so that she could look into my eyes. "Are you serious?"

Grinning, I stepped away from her. Then I went to the desk and pulled a small black box out from one of the drawers. "I bought this a week ago, thinking I was fed up with this nonsense of us trying to pretend we didn't care about each other. But the last time we made love, I decided that you weren't ready for me to give it to you yet."

I popped open the velvet box, and my heart swelled as Kia gasped, her eyes widening as she caught sight of the chocolate diamond set in platinum.

"I thought it matched the color of your eyes," I murmured as I started going down on one knee.

"Wait...hold on." Kia reached for her jeans, but I swatted her hands away.

"Stop that. I like you naked." I chuckled as I knelt, offering the ring up to Kia. "Kia Nash, love of my life and the most beautiful woman I have ever known...will you make me the happiest man on earth and be my wife?"

Tears filled Kia's eyes as she carefully took the ring from the box and slid it onto her finger. "It's a perfect fit," she whispered.

"Is that a yes?" I grinned up at her, happy as hell.

Laughing, she dropped to her knees and threw her arms around me. "Yes!" she cried, raining kisses down all over my face. "Yes, Hunter, I'll be your wife."

And I claimed her mouth in another bone-melting kiss, secure in the knowledge that Daniel was finally going to be avenged when we took all the evidence we had on that fucker Bradley, siccing the authorities on him. And I was finally settling down with the only woman I'd ever truly loved. I quietly acknowledged the reminder that, sometimes, you didn't know how much you were going to miss someone until they were back in your arms again. I'd just have to make sure I kept my arms around her for the rest of her days.

IF YOU LOVED HUNTER, YOU'RE going to devour Grumpy Special Ops Bear. Get more info here—>

GET A FREE SEDONA VENEZ BOOK!

https://sedonavenez.com/free-book

WANT FREE SEDONA VENEZ BOOKS?

Sign up for Sedona Venez's Newsletter and receive FREE BOOKS. In addition to the free stories, you will also get special pricing, exclusive previews and news of new releases.

GET A FREE SEDONA VENEZ BOOK!

Join Sedona's mailing list to be the first to know of new releases, free books, special prices and other author giveaways.

https://sedonavenez.com/free-book

ABOUT THE AUTHOR

USA TODAY BESTSELLING AUTHOR SEDONA VENEZ lives in New York City with her hot ex-military hubby—hooah—and their fur babies. She loves writing sizzling, sexy intricate stories about strong but broken characters who push limits, overcome their fears and risk it all for love.

Sedona loves to connect with readers!
www.sedonavenez.com